MOB TIES 5

SAYNOMORE

Lock Down Publications and Ca$h Presents
MOB TIES 5
A Novel by *SAYNOMORE*

Lock Down Publications
P.O. Box 944
Stockbridge, Ga 30281
www.lockdownpublications.com

Copyright 2022 by SAYNOMORE
Mob Ties 5

First Edition January 2022
Printed in the United States of America

This is a work of fiction. Names, characters, places, and incidents either are products of the author's imagination or are used fictitiously. Any similarity to actual events or locales or persons, living or dead, is entirely coincidental.

Lock Down Publications
Like our page on Facebook: Lock Down Publications @
www.facebook.com/lockdownpublications.ldp

Book interior design by: **Shawn Walker**
Edited by: **Nuel Uyi**

Stay Connected with Us!

Text **LOCKDOWN** to 22828 to stay up-to-date with new releases, sneak peaks, contests and more…

Thank you!

Submission Guideline.

Submit the first three chapters of your completed manuscript to ldpsubmissions@gmail.com, subject line: Your book's title. The manuscript must be in a .doc file and sent as an attachment. Document should be in Times New Roman, double spaced and in size 12 font. Also, provide your synopsis and full contact information. If sending multiple submissions, they must each be in a separate email.

Have a story but no way to send it electronically? You can still submit to LDP/Ca$h Presents. Send in the first three chapters, written or typed, of your completed manuscript to:

LDP: Submissions Dept
P.O. Box 944
Stockbridge, Ga 30281

DO NOT send original manuscript. Must be a duplicate.

Provide your synopsis and a cover letter containing your full contact information.

Thanks for considering LDP and Ca$h Presents.

You can get much further with a kind word and a gun than you can with a kind word alone
—Al Capone

Prologue

"Welcome home, Red Invee," Masi said.

Jamila gave a faint smile. "Thank you. It's good to be home, Masi."

"Do you want me to call a meeting with the other families?" asked Masi.

Jamila turned her head, looked at Masi and licked her lips.

"No, I don't want to do that yet. We'll have a meeting later this week. Before I do anything, take me to see Lorenzo." Jamila didn't say another word as they rode in the limo. The limousine pulled up to a red brick house. The driver got out, walked to the back of the limo, and opened Jamila's door so that she could step out of the vehicle. Jamila looked around, waiting for Muscle and Masi to walk in front of her first. As they walked around the back of the house, Jamila saw Lorenzo standing next to the grill. She couldn't help but look at Lorenzo with a smile on her face. When Lorenzo saw Jamila, he smiled back at her. She walked up to Lorenzo, then gave him long hug and a kiss on the cheek.

"I've missed you so much, Jamila," he said.

"No, Lorenzo, I missed you more. So are you one hundred percent strong to come back to the family, Lorenzo?"

"Yes, I am. I was just waiting on you to come home."

"Well, I'm home now, and it's time for bodies to be fished out of the Hudson River. But, first things first, I want a meeting with all the families in a few days. Also, I want you back at the restaurant with me and Tasha. Masi and Muscle will be at *Destiny's*. Dro will have *Passion's*, and we will figure out who we'll put at the waste plant."

"What about Symone?" asked Lorenzo.

"Lorenzo, it's been five years since I went shopping. I think it's time to go get some new jewelry. What do you think about that?" Jamila smiled at Lorenzo when she asked that question.

Lorenzo said, "I think it's time to go shopping then."

"I'm glad you agree. So, Lorenzo, are you gonna make me a plate of food?

"Yeah, I got you."

"Lorenzo, I just did five years. I want everything on that plate."

"Say less, Queen."

Chapter One

Jamila stepped out of her limo in front of Panache Fine Jewelry. She had a pair of black red bottom shoes, and a pair of faded blue jeans with rips on it. The jeans hugged her thighs, hips, and ass. She completed the ensemble with a black polo shirt alongside a blue and white Pelle Pelle jacket. Her hair was in curls, and a pair of black shades covered her eyes. She looked back at Lorenzo, Masi, Muscle, and Tasha. Muscle and Masi walked in front of her and opened the door to the jewelry shop. Lorenzo and Tasha walked behind her as she walked into Panache Fine. Jamila looked around; it was beautiful inside. The walls were painted red and gold. The carpet itself had red and gold stripes. There were eight shelves displaying jewelry.

"Lorenzo, it's beautiful in here. What do you think?"

"It would look better with Symone's blood on the walls."

A security guard walked over to them.

"Hello, how are you all doing today?" he asked. "Mr. Halo isn't here right now, but our assistant manager—Kimberly—will be right with you."

"Thank you," Jamila replied.

Jamila looked at Masi, and winked at him. Masi walked back to the front of the jewelry store where the security guard was standing. Tasha walked over to the first shelf as Kimberly was hanging up the phone.

"I'm sorry. I had a phone call I had to take, but welcome to Panache. How may I help you?"

At that point, Jamila snapped her fingers. At the same time, Masi and Tasha pulled their guns out. Masi put his gun to the security guard's head, telling him: "Don't be a hero, fuck up and die. Trust me, I have no problem killing a motherfucker. I done put a lot of faces on t-shirts."

Jamila walked up to Kimberly and looked back at Masi with his gun to the security guard's head. "Muscle, lock the door and turn the sign around from *open* to *close*. Masi, you can walk him this way. Kimberly, if you don't mind, you can walk us to the back."

Kimberly looked scared as Tasha had the gun to her head.

"Kimberly, do I have to ask you again?"

Tasha pressed the gun to her head when Jamila said that.

"No. No, please do not hurt me."

"Lorenzo, go get all the security video tapes and cut the cameras off. Muscle, tie them both up in those chairs over there."

"I don't know who the fuck y'all are, but do you know whose jewelry shop this is?" asked the security guard.

Jamila took her glasses off her face and said: "Let me tell you who I am, and why I don't give a fuck about Symone Rose, and let these be the last words you hear. My name is Jamila LaCross." When she said that, his eyes got as big as half dollar coin. "And that's why I don't give a fuck about no Symone Rose. Muscle, kill him." He was at a loss for words when she said that. Before he could blink an eye, Muscle shot him in the head at point-blank range; his body flew backwards, taking the seat with him as he hit the floor. Jamila looked at Kimberly. Masi was watching the front door, while Tasha was watching Lorenzo's back. Jamila sat down and crossed her legs as she watched Kimberly. "So, Kimberly, can you tell me where Mr. Halo went?" With tears in her eyes and a shaky voice, Kimberly was shivering out of control. Kimberly looked at Jamila. "He's at the casino. He had a meeting today."

"And what time are you expecting him back, Kimberly?"

"No later than five." Jamila looked at her watch, and saw that it was three forty-five p.m. She stood up, looked to the back room, and saw Lorenzo coming back with the video tapes.

"Did you cut the cameras off, Lorenzo?"

"Yeah, I did. I have all the video tapes right here, Jamila."

"Good, Kimberly, have you ever shot a gun before?"

Kimberly looked at Jamila and Lorenzo with tears coming down her face. "No."

"Well, today you are gonna shoot a gun, Kimberly. Tasha, give her your gun." Tasha walked up to Kimberly and handed her the gun. Jamila walked up behind Kimberly and laid her hand on her shoulder. "Now sweetheart, here's the test—the question is, *do you live or die?*" Holding the gun in her hand, Kimberly was more scared than she'd ever been in her life. "Kimberly, now what I want you to do is point the gun at the security guard's head and pull the trigger two times. I want his blood on your hands too. If you do this, you live. If you don't, you die." Jamila took two steps back and watched as Kimberly got up from the chair. Kimberly looked back at Jamila, pointed the gun at the security guard and shot him twice in the head. Masi walked up her and took the gun from her with rag in his hand. "Kimberly, come sit back down," Jamila said. Jamila watched as Kimberly sat down.

"Now Kimberly, here's the deal, this gun has your fingerprints on it, so that means you killed him. So I don't think you should open back up until Mr. Halo comes back from his meeting. Let him know Red Invee sends her best wishes. Do you understand why I'm telling you this, Kimberly?"

"Yes, I do."

"Good." Jamila looked at her one last time as she walked off, leaving her in the back with the dead security guard.

"Lorenzo, take me to *Jelani's* now," Jamila said as she walked off.

SAYNOMORE

Chapter Two

Symone was walking down stairs at the casino flanked by Iceman and Halo. Halo was telling Symone that Jamila was out of prison.

"What does that mean to me, Halo?"

"I'm just saying she might come at us."

"Halo, that bitch bleed just like we do. I give no fucks about her. Iceman, how is the income looking on your end?"

"Good. We good on my end. Everything is at one hundred percent."

"Good, I want Pistol to send some of his girls over here. I think it's about time you become a pimp. You think you can do that?"

"I'ma put their ass on the track, and they better not skip a beat."

"That's what I want to hear. I'll call Pistol tomorrow and let him know."

"I'll be waiting to hear from you, Ms. Rose." Iceman opened the casino doors and walked Symone out of the casino to the limo that was out front waiting for her. He opened the back door for her and Halo to step in. Once they were inside, he waited for the limo to pull off before walking back into the casino. Symone rolled down her window as she lit a Black and Mild. "Halo, our numbers are up from all our establishments. Iceman was the confirmation we needed. As for Red Invee, she knows her place. And if she do hit us, we just have to hit her harder. But, what we need to do now is—focus on our empire, Halo. You have four jewelry stores in Brooklyn that I need you to run with an iron fist. I'll have Man, B.R., and J. Mitch put in all the dirty work, but I need you, Lola, Iceman, Pistol and Perk-G to stay clean. One thing that I've learned is, someone is always watching."

"You are right, that's why we need friends that can sit at tables we can't. I'm talking about judges, lawyers, D.A.'s, and cops. We need to be able to win in the streets and in the courtrooms."

"You make a good point, Halo. I'll get on that tomorrow. I have someone who can put that in motion for me."

Symone put her Black and Mild out as their limo came to a stop. A few seconds later, her door opened, then she and Halo stepped out.

"Halo, why is the store closed?"

"I don't know. Kimberly is supposed to be here."

Symone looked around, pulled her gun out and held it at her side. Halo opened the door, then looked back at Symone. Once inside, Symone looked around, but there was nothing broken or touched.

"Halo, where is Kimberly or Kevin?"

"I don't know. This isn't like Kimberly."

"There's a light on in the back room, Halo."

Symone and Halo had their guns out as they walked toward the back room.

"Fuck me, Symone! Kimberly, are you alright?" Halo said as he ran over to her. She balled up in a corner, crying. He placed his gun on the floor as he kneeled next to her. Symone just looked at her and Kevin's dead body. His face was gone, and there was blood everywhere. She looked at Kimberly as Halo held her. Halo held up her head, and looked in her eyes. "Kimberly, tell me, what happened? Symone, would you pass me the tissue on my desk, please?" Symone passed Halo the tissue and watched as he wiped Kimberly's face. "Kimberly, tell me, what happened?" he asked again.

"A lady came in with two guys and a female. She said her name was Red Invee." Halo looked at Symone when she said the name. "Kimberly, tell me everything that happened."

"I don't remember everything, I was so scared, but I remember a gun to my face. She said something to Kevin and had one of the guys shoot him in the face and then she had me shoot him in the face. She took the gun back from me and told me to tell you that *Red Invee sends her best wishes*."

Halo looked up at Symone and asked, "What do you think?"

"It's time to call Man and B.R. Let me talk to Kimberly for a second."

As Halo got up and walked to his desk, Kimberly was still on the floor.

"Kimberly, everything is gonna be alright. I promise you that." Symone looked at Halo and pointed her gun at Kimberly. All at once, gun blasts bounced off the walls as Symone shot Kimberly six times in the chest, killing her.

"Halo, go lock the front door and pull the truck around back."

"Symone, why did you kill her?" Halo asked.

"She was a weak link. She said Red Invee has the gun that had her fingerprints on it, and she will use that against us, to come after us. We don't know what Kimberly would have told her if she felt her life was in danger, or if she would have talked to the police. It's necessary that she dies, to save us and this family in the long run. I don't give a fuck about Red Invee. She's just another bitch to me. She thinks she's the queen. Well, Halo, I'm coming for the crown. I want Man and B.R. to be here twenty-four-seven from now on."

***

Muscle and Masi were fifteen feet back, watching the scene as Jamila paid her respects to Frankie. Jamila kneeled over Frankie's grave as she placed two roses—red and white—on his grave.

"Frankie, it's been six years and I miss you so much. I remember the first day we met. I would have never guessed that you'd be a second father in my life. Sometimes I wish I would have never asked you to help me get close to Felipe if I knew your life was the price I would have to pay for killing him. I miss you. I miss our talks, and our walks around the park. But I promise you, everything that you ever showed me or told me is locked away in my heart and my soul. I know you looking down on me every day as a guardian angel. I just wish we had more time. I just feel that you were taken away from me too soon." Jamila had tears coming down her face as she talked to Frankie with her head on his tombstone.

"Anyway, I have to go. But I will send a few more people to see you before this is over. And the Scott family is at the top of my list, right next to Symone, and when I send them to you, kill their ass again. Fuck sleeping in peace. I want them killed in death again." Jamila kissed her two fingers and touched his tombstone. "Sleep in peace." Jamila got up, brushed the dust off her knees, then walked back to Muscle and Masi.

"You ready, Red Invee?"

"Yeah, Muscle. Take me to *Jelani's*."

Chapter Three

Symone was sipping on a glass of wine as she was walking the floor in her office at the casino. She stopped in front of the security monitors, watching the casino floor. She watched Iceman talk to Joe Scott and his two men. She watched as they made their way to her office, then she walked back to her desk and took a seat. She heard two knocks on the door before Iceman walked in with Joe Scott and his men. "Ms. Rose, Joe Scott is here to see you."

"Iceman, if you don't mind, would you please get Mr. Scott and his associates something to drink? Water, wine, or something stronger."

"No, thank you, Ms. Rose," Joe Scott replied. "No need for any drink,"

"Scott, how may I help you?"

"I heard about what happened with Red Invee last week, how she killed one of your guys."

"Yes, that was unexpected. But trust me, I do have a plan to pay her back for that one."

"Well, I'm here to help you with that."

Symone tilted her head when he said that.

"What do you mean, Mr. Scott?"

Iceman walked back to the table with a bottle of Cîroc and four glasses. He poured everybody a double shot.

"Mr. Scott, I would take it as disrespect if you didn't have a drink with me. After all, you are in my establishment."

Joe Scott took the shot that Iceman poured, tapped his glass and drank it. Symone watched as he took his shot.

"Mr. Scott, continue what you were saying now."

"Last night, off of Bayview, one of the LaCross boys was down there talking with a few guys from the Lenacci family about how she killed one of your guards and how she's looking for you to put your head on her shelf as a trophy."

"Mr. Scott, what was his name?"

"Corey. Does that name sound familiar?"

"I know who he is. Do you know where I can find him?"

"I sure do. He's already waiting for you. Field forty-three, about twenty-five minutes away from here."

Symone looked at Iceman and said to him: "Get the car ready. We're about to take a ride. Tell Pistol I need him to take the ride with us as well."

Symone looked at Iceman as he had the double-barreled shotgun in his hand. He had a cold look on his face. She knew he was ready to kill somebody. She looked at Pistol as he held two Glock nines in his hands. He had his head down, waiting for whatever to come his way. Symone felt the bumps on the road they were on. As she looked out the window, all she saw was a cornfield that was ten miles long. After ten minutes, the limo came to a stop. Symone looked at Iceman as her limo door opened. Iceman got out first, then Symone and Pistol. When Symone got out the limo and looked around, she saw Joe Scott and three of his men a little way up in front of her. She saw there was a man on his knees with a paper bag over his head next to them.

"Come on, y'all—Symone, he's right there waiting on you," Joe said. Symone walked up to him and pulled the bag off his head. He looked up at Symone.

"Hello, Corey. I know you didn't want to see me on these terms, but here we are." Corey looked at Iceman walking up to him with the double-barreled shotgun in his hands.

"Why're you looking at him? You know I'm gonna kill you, Corey. You know how this is gonna end, with your body in that hole over there." Symone pulled her phone out and started recording the whole thing. Corey knew how this was gonna end when he saw Symone. He knew he was dead. He didn't even beg for his life. He just watched her as she was recording everything. Then the shotgun blasted, sending Corey's body flying into the hole he was kneeling by. Iceman shot him two more times when he was in the hole. Symone put her phone in her pocket and walked over to Joe Scott.

"So you think she's gonna come after you now, Rose?"

"I'm not gonna give her a chance. I'm sending my shooters after her tonight."

"Let me know if you need me, Rose."

20

"Mr. Scott, I need you out of the picture so nothing comes back your way, but keep playing your part for me."

Symone walked over to Joe Scott, and gave him a kiss on the cheek before going back to her limo. Iceman looked at her, as she forwarded the video to Lorenzo's phone and typed a message that read: *Give Red Invee my best regards.*

"Pistol and Iceman, make sure you watch the doors to the casino and the strip club very carefully, because Red Invee is going to come at us very soon. I'm gonna call Perk-G and have him make up ten keys for the both of you while Lola pick up the deposits. Make sure y'all are ready when she gets there." Iceman and Pistol nodded at Symone. Symone put her phone up, pulled out a Black and Mild and lit it as they drove back to the jewelry shop.

***

Jamila was standing next to her birdcage when Larenzo walked into her office.

"Jamila, I have something you need to see."

"What is that, Lorenzo?"

Lorenzo walked up to Jamila and handed her his phone. Jamila watched the video of Corey being killed, then she read the message.

"When did you get this, Lorenzo?"

"About two hours ago, Jamila. She just killed him."

Jamila handed him back the phone. "Call a meeting. I want everyone here tomorrow at one p.m., and see if you can find out where they killed him at so we can give his body to his family."

SAYNOMORE

Chapter Four

The lights were dim, but bright enough for the people to see each other and dance. Vinnie sat in the VIP section, talking on the phone. He had three body guards standing outside the VIP section. He was smoking his cigar. When he looked to the left, he saw Chris Gambino walking up to the VIP section. Vinnie tapped the rope to let his bodyguard know to let Gambino in.

"Vinnie, I see you doing the same thing Tony used to do. Sitting in the corner of the VIP, talking on the phone, with three body guards watching over you."

"Chris, sometimes it's good to follow old patterns. So, tell me, what brings you by?"

"Just to talk," said Chris.

"About what?" asked Vinnie.

"Rose and Joe," replied Chris.

"What about them?"

"Now that the Queen Don is out of prison, how do you think she's gonna take it that Joe Scott is allies with Rose?"

"I don't know," Vinnie said as he pulled on his cigar.

"Word got back to me, Vinnie, that Red Invee paid Rose a visit and killed one of her guys."

"I did hear that, Chris."

"But did you hear the second part of the story, Vinnie?"

"No, Chris. Tell me the second part of this story."

"Rose took one of Red Invee's guys to the cornfield and put a double-barreled shotgun to his face and blew it off, then dumped his body in a hole."

"Now that I did not hear."

"If you ain't hear that, then I know you didn't hear that it was one of Joe Scott's men that kidnapped him and took him to the cornfield for Rose."

Vinnie put his cigar down and looked at Chris.

"Now by him doing that, he crossed a line and his head is definitely about to be on the chopping block. Do any of the other families know about this, Chris?"

"No, just our two families as of right now."

"Chris, Joe took a gamble, but what he doesn't know is where we stand at with the Queen Don. If she calls, then we move. You think he would have learned his place on the food chain. He should know a lion ain't humble in the jungle and a bear can't kill a gorilla." Vinnie picked up his glass, took a sip and sat it back down, then picked up his cigar and lit it again.

"You know what, Chris? Let's do Red Invee a favor, and find out who kidnapped her guy and brought him to Rose. Let's get them and bring them to Red Invee so she knows whose side we're playing on."

Chris knocked on the table twice before getting up to leave.

"Chris," Vinnie called out.

Chris stopped, turned around and looked at Vinnie.

"Let's try and do this quietly. I want to keep this under the covers."

Chris nodded and walked off.

Chapter Five

Jamila walked into *Jelani's*. She had on a white shirt, black, knee-length leather skirt, and black open-toed shoes. Her hair was in curls that came down to her shoulders. She was wearing a pair of Louis Vuitton sunglasses as she walked past one of her waiters.

"Damn, you sure look smokin' hot and sexy, Ms. LaCross," the waiter said. Jamila stopped and looked at him, not saying a word. She looked into his light brown eyes and deep dark waves. He was olive-skinned. He had a cute smile, and his lips looked soft. He was six feet tall and well-built. He looked to weigh about two hundred and twenty pounds.

"Thank you. Can you bring a bottle of Moët up to my office?"

"Yes, Ms. LaCross."

"OK. I'll be waiting for it." Jamila walked off, headed towards the elevator, not looking back. Once in her office, she went to the sound system and put on TLC's '*Red Light Special*'. She walked over to her sliding doors so that she could feel the warm breeze blowing in from outside. That's when she heard a knock at the door. She walked to the door and opened it.

"Come in and put the bottle on the table over there."

Jamila stepped to the side to let him in. She closed her office door, locked it, and walked up to him.

"What is your name?"

"Michael."

"What do they call you?"

"Styles."

Jamila picked up the bottle of Moët and poured herself a full glass. "Styles, who am I?" she asked him.

"Jamila LaCross," he answered.

"And what do they call me?"

"Red Invee."

"You know, Styles, I have killed more people than the boogey-man himself. In the worst ways. So I'm gonna ask you a few questions, and I want you to be honest with me. Do I make myself clear?"

"Yes."

"Good. Now have a seat." Michael looked at her and sat down at the table. Jamila looked at him as she took another sip of her drink.

"So, tell me, Styles, how should I take it when I walk in my place of business and one of my employees come to me flirting with me in front of other employees? Do you think that was appropriate? Now what if someone would have heard you?"

"I'm sorry. I didn't mean it that way."

"So tell me, how did you mean it?"

"Not in a disrespectful way, Ms. LaCross."

"Since you like using your tongue, don't worry, you're gonna use it."

Jamila got up, grabbed his hand, then walked him to the couch in her office and pushed him down on it. She sat next to him and placed her leg on the back of the couch.

Michael looked at her.

"Put your face between my thighs and eat my pussy until I tell you to stop."

Michael looked at her as he lowered his head. She grabbed his head and pressed his face against her pussy. Michael placed his tongue inside of her, and she started rubbing her pussy all over his face. Jamila put her other leg on his back, moaning faintly, as Michael made his tongue go in circles inside of her. He took his arms and wrapped them around her legs, as he licked and sucked all over her. Jamila put her hands on his head and wrapped her legs around his neck.

"Don't stop, keep going, lick on my clit, do it now."

Michael felt Jamila cumming in his mouth.

"Oh shit, oh shit, open your mouth wide and you better catch it all." Jamila grabbed his head and pushed her pussy over his mouth. She let out a scream as she squirted in his mouth. Michael had his mouth over her pussy, trying to catch every drop. Jamila picked his head up and was looking at him. He had her juices all over his face running down his chin.

"You got all of that out of me, so you are going to swallow it. Right?" Michael nodded, and Jamila watched as he swallowed everything.

"Michael, go get a drink over there on the table."

Michael poured himself a glass of Moët as Jamila watched him. Jamila walked up behind him.

"Did you like that?"

He looked at her. "Yes, I did."

"Good. Because when I call you, be ready. Now, wipe your face then you can leave. And, Michael, if I hear one word about this, I'll have your tongue taken out of your mouth." Jamila looked at him and walked to the bathroom.

SAYNOMORE

Chapter Six

The room was quiet, a yellow light shining off the wall. There were four families waiting for Jamila to show up. Vinnie Lenacci, Chris Gambino, Kevin Deniro, and Paul Landon. Everyone looked when the door opened up and Jamila walked in with Lorenzo. Everyone stood up when they saw her. Jamila took her seat at the head of the table.

"Gentlemen, it's good to see you all in one place again."

"We are all glad that you are home, Red Invee," Vinnie Lenacci said.

"Thank you, Mr. Lenacci. It's good to be home. First, I wanna thank all of you for staying loyal to me in my time of absence. I see we are missing Joe Scott from his seat, and Glen Teliono from his seat. Can someone tell me why is that?"

"Joe Scott decided to make friends with Symone Rose, and from my understanding, they are allies now. I don't know where Glen Teliono is."

"Thanks for letting me know that, Mr. Gambino. For the last decade there have been wars in these streets, and we have all lost millions of dollars at this table. Everyone here should know that I'm gonna strike back at the Rose family and the Scott family for their disloyalty. Just like I did the Zimmerman family, and look—there's an empty seat right there, and it's been that way for six years now. But we're gonna do something different now. We're gonna take the food out of their mouths. No one at this table is to supply Joe Scott. He is to get no aid and assistance for anything. I want Brooklyn to be as dry as the Sahara Desert. People from Brooklyn will have to come to Queens, the Bronx, Manhattan, Yonkers, and everywhere else for their work, and I'm also gonna take the food out of Rose's mouth as well. Don't worry about the Scott family. Right now, I want the Rose family to feel my pain."

"Red Invee, may I say something, please?"

"You have the table, Mr. Gambino." Mr. Gambino stood up, and placed both his hands on the table as he addressed everyone.

"We have had a lot of Dons, and Ms. LaCross—you are the only one who never asked for dues from us. You are giving us the best prices on one hundred percent pure cocaine. You help all of our families out in the courtrooms, one way or another, and you don't push your weight around. I've said all of this to say you'll forever have the loyalty of the Gambino family." Mr. Gambino took his seat after those words.

"Thank you, Mr. Gambino, for your kind words and your loyalty."

Mr. Lenacci stood up.

"Ms. LaCross, Mr. Gambino speaks the truth. No matter what our differences were in the past, to protect our families, you never changed. You always put the MOB first. Everyone at this table can say that. The Scott family chose the side they wanted to be on. They put Rose before the MOB and broke the rules by trying to kill the Queen Don. To add more insult on top of that, he helped kidnap one of your guys that Rose killed in the cornfield. So we at this table have something for you, Ms. LaCross."

"And what is it that you have for me?"

Vinnie looked at his men and nodded. All eyes were on him when he walked off. Jamila watched as he came back through the doors with a man that had his hands tied behind his back and a bag over his head. He walked the man to a chair and sat him down in it.

"So who is this, Mr. Lenacci?"

"Spade. One of Joe Scott's men. He was the one who kidnapped your guy for Rose."

"Remove the bag." Jamila looked at him.

"So he's the one that had one of my brothers killed in my family?" Jamila got up as she continued to talk.

"So, tell me, Spade, why shouldn't I kill you?"

Spade lowered his head.

"I don't give a fuck if you kill me. Death been calling my name, and I been doing whatever Joe Scott ask me to do. So if he say fuck you, then I say fuck you."

Chris Gambino yelled: "Mind your fucking tongue. That's the Queen Don you talking to, boy!"

30

"No, it's OK. I like the fact that he speaks his mind. But let me tell you something, Spade, you killed yourself when you went against me. Put concrete around his feet and throw him in the Hudson. Alive. And make sure Joe follow you down there." Spade still had his head down. Jamila pulled her gun out in front of everyone and smacked him in the face with it.

"Pussy motherfucker. I want blocks on his feet, and I want him dumped in the Hudson. I ain't playing. Mr. Lenacci, thank you. Lorenzo, let's go." Jamila looked at everyone one last time before walking out the door.

***

A chill breeze was blowing over the Hudson. One could see the lights from the cars passing over the Hudson Bridge. The sky was pitch-black as the boat glided over the water.

"Mark, don't do it like this. Shoot me in the head, Nick. We've known each other for years."

"Spade, you put yourself in the situation you are in now and I'm not gonna put myself in the same situation you are in by trying to help you out."

"So you throwing away fifteen years of friendship for a nigger."

Nick looked at Mark. Mark grabbed Spade's arms while Nick grabbed his legs.

"I'll see both of y'all in hell!" Spades yelled as his body hit the water with a splash.

"Come on, Mark let's get the fuck outta here. I hate this water at night."

SAYNOMORE

Chapter Seven

"I'm not worried about Red Invee or nobody else. If anybody crosses the line, we strike. We have the Rose family backing us up, and we have control over Brooklyn." Joe Scott said those words as he smoked his cigar while talking to Pete. Joe sat behind his desk right before there was a knock at the door.

"Come in."

"Mr. Scott, this just came here for you."

Joe Scott reached his hand out as he received a small white box. He looked at it.

"Pete, I wonder what this is."

As he opened the box, he let out a shout.

"You gotta be fucking kidding me!"

"What you got there, Joe?" Pete asked.

"Spade's pinky ring and the picture of a fish. Pete, find out who killed him, and send them on a flight to see him."

Joe put the ring on his pinky finger, then kissed it.

"Pete, do what I just asked you to do, and be quick about it!" Joe watched as Pete walked out the door. Joe opened his desk drawer, pulled out two stress balls and started rotating them in his hand. He felt uneasy, knowing that Spade's body was at the bottom of the Hudson.

***

Oso's phone went off while he was in his Jacuzzi watching two females kiss each other and play with themselves for him. He reached and picked up his phone.

"Hello."

"Hello, Oso. Is this line safe to talk on?"

Oso looked at his phone to see the number calling him.

Then he continued to talk.

"Red Invee, no, let me call you right back."

Jamila hung up, picked up her drink and took a sip right before Oso called her back. Jamila picked up the phone and walked to the front of the yatch she was on.

"Red Invee, it's good to hear your voice."

"Likewise, Oso. How has business been for you?"

"Good, very good."

"That's good to hear, Oso. I'm calling about that good business you've been having."

"What about the good business? I'm listening." Oso pulled on his cigar.

"Oso, is the enemy of my enemy, my enemy as well?"

"I don't understand the question that you're asking me, Red Invee."

"Oso, to my understanding, you are doing business with Rose."

"I am. She is your sister."

"She is my sister, just like Morwell was your brother, but you had to do what you had to do, right? Here's the thing, Oso, I can't continue to buy from you if you are going to supply my enemy. Here's my question, Oso, do you want to throw away ten years of loyal business with myself and others from my city because of a new relationship you have with my little sister?"

Oso pulled on his cigar and blew the smoke out.

"Red Invee, out of the respect that we have for each other, I will cut off all dealings with Symone Rose. But, I also want you to know I did not know what was going on in New York City."

"I understand and I respect that, Oso, and I also want to thank you for respecting our relationship. So, when am I gonna see you again, Oso?"

"I can pay you a visit in the next few weeks."

"I can't wait to see you."

"Likewise. I'll see you in the next few weeks, Red Invee."

Oso hung up and made his way to the two females in his Jacuzzi, where they were still sucking and kissing each other. Oso took the hand of one of the girls, pulled her to him and started kissing her, while the other female went underwater and started sucking on him. As he closed his eyes, still kissing this girl, the other girl came from under the water and started sucking on his neck.

"Ladies, come on, let's take this to my bedroom."

***

Lorenzo walked up to Jamila at the front of the yatch, and handed Jamila her drink.

"So what did he say?"

"As of right now, Rose does not have a supplier. I want Masi and Muscle to go by the House of Diamonds and see how the layout is inside. I want to stop every source of income she has coming in."

"I'll get on that right away." Lorenzo turned around and walked off, leaving Jamila looking at the sea as she felt the warm breeze on her skin.

***

Symone walked into the restaurant and saw two men sitting at a table in the back.

"Hello, gentlemen."

Both of the men got up to shake Symone's hand.

"Symone Rose, it's good to finally meet you. My name is Ross, and my friend here is Mosley. So tell me, what can I do for you Ms. Rose?"

"I was told you could help me make friends, Mr. Ross."

Symone watched as he took a sip of his drink.

"I can help you make friends, Ms. Rose, but everything comes with a price. Now this is what I can offer you: I have two District Attorneys and one Judge, and we're asking ten thousand a month. Rest assured you'll walk every time."

"Mr. Ross, can I smoke in here?"

"Sure, you can."

Symone pulled out a Black and Mild, lowered her head and lit it.

"I can do ten thousand a month, Mr. Ross, but Mr. Scott told me I'd be getting cops too." Symone watched as both men pulled out badges and put them on the table.

"Who do you think we are?"

Symone smiled. "So what are your limits?"

"I can answer that question with this one, what is your price, Ms. Rose?"

"We'll talk about it when that time comes. So, I'm only protected in Brooklyn?"

"Only in Brooklyn."

"That works for me. Do you know where Panache Fine Jewelry store is?"

"Yeah, I know where it's at."

"Good, come by there tomorrow after three p.m."

"We'll be there," the men chorused.

"I'll see you then, gentlemen." Symone put her Black and Mild out, and got up from the table. She walked back to her limo where Pistol was waiting for her.

"Are you ready, Ms. Rose?"

"Yes. Take me to see Perk-G."

Chapter Eight

Detective Green sat at his desk, rubbing his head, looking over the files he had on the Rose family.

"What am I missing? What don't I see?" Detective Green asked himself. He got up and walked down the hall to Detective Hall's office. After two knocks on the door, he heard Hall say: "Come in."

Detective Hall looked up from his table as Detective Green walked in. "Look what the wind blew in." Hall got up and shook Detective Green's hand. "So how can I help you, Green?"

Detective Green sat down and looked at Hall.

"I've been working on this Rose case day and night. There are a few things I can't figure out. It's just—"

"Green, sorry to cut you off, but do you know why no other detective took on that case? Do you know why Chief Tadem didn't want no part of it?"

"No, nobody told me and I never asked."

Detective Hall got up, went to his door and looked out both ways to see if anybody was standing there. He closed his door, then went and shut his window. Detective Green was looking at him, and wondering why he was moving like that.

"Look, Green, this goes nowhere. This stays between us."

"OK. You have my word. I won't tell a soul."

"Listen to me very clearly. Eight years ago, Jamila's name came across Chief Tadem's desk. The case was about a black female don. He blew it off. Not just him, everybody. It was a joke to us. You do remember the *"Red Summer."* The newspaper was calling it *the worst Mafia war ever in the history of New York City.*"

"Yeah, I remember that. I remember all of that."

"Good, but what you didn't know, and what you wouldn't have read in the newspaper is this—the reason the D.A. Moore and his driver were killed is because he was pushing the case against the LaCross family, and the Landon family after Mr. Deniro was killed on a prison transport bus. You know how you have that pyramid with Symone Rose on the top?"

"Yeah."

"Well, Detective Boatman had that pyramid with her sister Jamila LaCross a.k.a. Red Invee on the top. Lenacci family had a lot of back-ups and made men who supported them. Do you remember Tony Lenacci, *the Boss of all Bosses*? After Red Invee killed him, she killed everybody around him—Starting with Mayor Oakland, and she didn't care who was around him because if she did, there wouldn't have been two dead cops and three dead security guards. See, Jamila had her own pyramid, and everyone she had on it from the top to the bottom was killed. Let me throw a few names at you: Mayor Oakland, D.A. Moore, Jatavious Stone, Mr. Deniro, drug lord Felipe Conway, and many more, but there was one she let live because she liked his wife and children. And do you know who she let live?"

"Who?"

"Chief Tadem."

Detective Green looked Detective Hall directly in the eyes.

"Chief Tadem came home, and Jamila had his wife and kids on the couch. Before he could blink an eye, two guns were pointed at this head. She told him, *'Leave the case alone and live a long happy healthy life with your wife and kids, and if you bring this case up again, you'll only be able to talk to D.A. Moore face to face with your wife and kids in the afterlife.'* Her men took the guns out of Chief Tadem's face, and she walked out the back door like she was never there. That's when reality hit us, that there was a black female don in New York City. Detective Boatman kept fishing in the wrong sea and got burned with *two and three*. Two bullets to the head and three to the chest."

"So all of this happened and we have proof? Why didn't we take her down?"

"Because she is protected, and when she walks out of the courtroom like John Gotti, then we have to worry about our families. Sometimes it's best to leave shit alone. Listen, Green, we live in two different worlds—us and the Mafia. They live in the shadows and we don't. They have friends that smile in our faces, friends we'll never recognize. Green, get out while you can."

"Hall, I can bring her ass down. I think I can prove that she's the one who killed Detective Boatman."

"Look, Green, I'm trying to save your ass. If you're not gonna listen to me or take my advice, at least put some money to the side for your family, 'cause—trust me—they're going to need it."

"Hall, I came here to ask you for your help."

"And I just gave it to you. Let me break it down like ABC and 123: *Drop the case and walk away*, because it's not gonna end like you think it is."

"Thanks, Hall." Detective Green got up and walked out of Hall's office. Once he closed the door, Detective Hall picked up the phone and made a call.

Chapter Nine

"Lorenzo, I need a shadow, someone I can count on, someone I can trust that I know can get the job done without an excuse."

"You already have Masi and Muscle, and don't forget Dro."

"I know who I have already, Lorenzo, and so does everyone else. I need an out-of-town killer, an out-of-town shooter. I need everyone to be in the police's eyesight at all times to keep them clean, but I still need the job done. That's why I need a shadow. And a new runner to make drops and pick-ups." Jamila drank her glass of water.

"I know two guys. They are brothers, from New Jersey. One is a real monster who takes pleasure in killing his victims, and the other one used to be a driver for Orlando Preston before he got killed. I'll make the call and see if they'll come see me."

"No, I don't want them nowhere near my place of business. Make the call, and we'll go see them. I remember Orlando Preston. How did he die again?

"The family that left '*The Seven*'—the Teliono family—set him up and had him whacked right after the New York Mets game. They had him killed in the parking lot, gunned down right before he got in his car."

Jamila walked to her birdcage.

"I see. Lorenzo, go make the call and let me know when I'll be able to meet our new friends."

***

There were two guards outside the gate on the pier. It was wet and damp outside. All they saw were headlights coming towards them. The light reflected off the wet pavement as the limo came to a stop at the gate. One of the guards walked over to the driver's window. The driver rolled the window down.

"Who are you here to see?"

"Chase Teliono."

"Who wants to see him?"

"Symone Rose."

"Hold on." The guard walked back to the gate, pulled out his phone and made a call as he watched the limo. A few seconds later, the gate opened and the guard waved for the limo to go inside. The limo pulled up to the warehouse doors. Another guard came out, holding an M-16. The driver got out, walked to the back of the limo, and opened the door for Symone. The guard watched as Iceman stepped out first, then Pistol. The guard had heard stories about Symone but tonight was the first time he'd seen her. When Symone stepped out the limo, she looked like a model. He watched her as she walked to the door.

"Right this way, Ms. Rose."

Symone walked in the room, where she saw four men standing around. Chase turned around and saw Symone standing between Iceman and Pistol.

"Ms. Rose it's a pleasure to finally meet you."

"Likewise, Mr. Teliono."

"So, tell me, Ms. Rose, what can I do for you?"

"I was thinking maybe we could help each other out. From my understanding, you pulled your family out of '*The Seven*', when Cobra was killed."

"Yes, I did, and I still didn't get my blood back from his death."

"See, that's the thing, Mr. Teliono, we shouldn't have to ask to get the blood back that was spilled from our family. We should just take it back, and that's what I bring to you today to this table."

Chase walked to his desk and sat on the edge of it, as he looked at Symone.

"I've heard stories about you, Symone—Red Invee's kid sister. You're the one striking fear in the hearts of the toughest killers in New York City. It's a delight talking to you face to face on my docks. So you're suggesting that we take our blood back? That would be an all-out chaotic war. Don't get me wrong, Ms. Rose. I've heard stories about you, but I've witnessed first-hand Red Invee's wrath when she killed off four of the Lenacci's top made men. She leaves me alone down here, so why should I bump heads with the Queen Don?"

"That's the thing, Mr. Teliono. Whose Don is she? It's not as if she's Queen of England." Symone started walking around Chase's office, and stopped at a map of New York City.

"Chase, right now Brooklyn is mine and I'm looking to take over the Bronx. If you help me, I'll help you get your blood back."

"So you're telling me two families are gonna go against five families?"

"No, I'm not telling you that. I'm telling you three families is gonna go against five families. We might be underdogs but if we cut the head off, the body will fall."

"So, you're telling me you are gonna kill Red Invee?"

"Yes. I'm telling you I'm gonna stand over her body, point my gun in her face and blow her fucking head off. Mr. Teliono, I'm offering you my hand today as a new beginning. Bear in mind that when you start something new, you have to get rid of the old."

"Let's just say I'm thinking about this. Who's the third family that will be standing next to us?"

Symone turned around and looked at him with a smile on her face.

"The Scott family will be backing us up as well."

Chase got up from his desk and walked to Symone.

"I'm gonna take a chance and walk on a limb with you. Please don't make me regret it."

"Mr. Teliono, that is something you won't have to worry about. I can assure you of that."

"So let's drink to a new trust founded on loyalty, Ms. Rose."

"Let's toast to trust, loyalty and honor, Mr. Teliono."

Chase walked to the bar and poured two drinks. He handed one to Symone. They tapped glasses and took their shots together.

"Mr. Teliono, I have to be going but I will be in touch with you."

"Take care, Ms. Rose. I look forward to hearing from you."

Symone nodded as she walked out the door back to her limo.

"Iceman and Pistol, I think I wanna kill Masi. And if I know Jamila, she'll have him at the hotel and he might be with Muscle.

Pistol, this is something I want you to get done, and if you can't get Masi, leave a body count."

"You don't have to worry about that, Ms. Rose. This will be like taking candy from a baby."

"That's what I like to here," said Symone, as she lowered her head and lit her Black and Mild, watching as Pistol cocked both of his Glock 40's.

Chapter Ten

Perk-G watched from the corner of the room as his workers put together twenty kilos of *red flame*. He had two crews of three females each—three counting up the kilos, and three counting the money that Lola brought. He got up and walked to the table as they were counting the money.

"Jessica, what is the count so far?"

"The count is three hundred thousand so far. We are placing all the ones, fives, tens, twenties, fifties, and hundreds all in their own separate stacks with the amount on top, and we still have those three duffle bags over there to count. We should be done by nine-thirty p.m. at the latest."

"OK. Let me know when you are done. April, how is it going over there on that table?"

"We only have three more kilos to wrap up and then we'll be done, Perk-G."

"April, make sure everything is airtight and compressed to the max." Perk-G walked off and called Halo. After two rings, he picked up.

"Yo, peace."

"Peace."

"This Perk-G calling to let you know everything is ready to be picked up."

"Copy that. Just hold everything till tomorrow. Rose don't want Lola picked up this late at night. I'll have her swing through tomorrow at four-thirty p.m., no later than five p.m."

"Copy. Everything will be on standby when she gets here."

"That's what I like to hear. I'll let her know, Perk-G."

"Copy." Perk-G hung up and walked back to the room to check on the girls. He sat back in the corner and rolled a blunt to smoke until they were done.

***

Jamila didn't talk much as the limo drove down the long, dark road while the raindrops hit the roof of the car.

"Lorenzo, what can you tell me about Young Cap?"

"Everything you need to know is right here." He passed her a folder with the dude's information inside. She looked at his name—Derrick Strong. She opened the folder and saw his nickname: *Young Cap*. According to Young Cap's details in the folder, he was black, thirty-six years of age, and weighed 300 pounds, although his height wasn't stated in the file. He was from New Jersey. His M.O. included murder, kidnapping, aggravated assault and battery.

"Lorenzo, it says here he went to jail for killing a house of five. Mother, father, brother, son, and daughter. He went to trial and beat all charges against him. How did he do that?"

"The last day of his trial, right before it began, the judge got a phone call from his wife when he was in his chambers. He picked up, and there was a man on the other end of the phone whose voice he heard. And all the voice said was '*Derrick Strong better not get convicted. He'd better walk. I'm gonna send you some pictures*'. Then he got the pictures with his family tied up with a chainsaw targeted at them, and I think you know the rest of the story. Derrick Strong walked out the courtroom a free man. Nobody could believe it."

"Lorenzo, what does *Young Cap* stand for? It doesn't say in here."

Lorenzo looked at her and smiled. "It stands for: *You Only Understand Niggas Gravesites Collect And Punish*."

"You know what, Lorenzo? I think I'm gonna like this Young Cap. I can't wait to meet him."

Jamila laid the folder down on the seat as the limo came to a stop. The driver ran to her door and opened it up. He had an umbrella waiting for her when she stepped out. Jamila looked around. She saw a bunch of bushes, trees and a muddy road. She saw an old log house. Lorenzo stepped out the limo and was standing next to her.

"Lorenzo, where the fuck you got me at?"

"If I had to give it a name, I would say: *Hell*."

Jamila and Lorenzo walked up to the house where they heard the cries of a man. Jamila looked at Lorenzo and pulled her gun out.

"I really hope I don't have to kill a motherfucker tonight, Lorenzo."

Lorenzo had his gun out as they walked around the side of the house to the shed. When they looked inside, there was a man tied naked to a wooden X-shaped cross. Jamila just watched as he was being tortured while the man in front of him branded him over and over again. The metal was so hot it was the color orange.

"I bet you ain't think you'd be tied to a wooden X tonight. Let me tell you this. I get everyone I say I'm gonna get." Young Cap pulled the metal out of the burning coals and looked at it. His victim couldn't hold his head up. He was too weak. Cap said without looking back: "Lorenzo, I'll be right with you and the Queen Don." Young Cap looked at the burning metal, and placed it back in the hot coals. He looked at the table, picked up a saw, and walked to the man on the wooden X. He grabbed his head with his left hand, and with his right hand he cut his head off. Blood was everywhere. Jamila just watched him. Young Cap took the man's head, opened a door and threw it in there. Then he took the body off the wooden X, dragged it to the same door and threw it in there.

"Ms. LaCross, I'm sorry you had to witness that, but I had to get the job done. It would have been longer if you hadn't shown up."

"I truly understand. Sometimes you have to do what you have to do no matter who's around. Mr. Cap, I asked Lorenzo to reach out to you for me because I want to offer you a job. From what I just saw, you are the perfect man for the job I need done."

Jamila looked at Cap as he washed his hands off in the sink.

"So, who do you want killed?"

"Does it matter, Mr. Cap?"

"No."

"Good. Now these are the rules on how I want the job done."

Cap turned around and looked at Jamila. "What are your rules?"

"Nothing comes back to me, and I need you to move like a shadow. If you can follow these two rules, I will make you a very wealthy man."

"When do you need the job done?"

"Just be on standby when I call, Mr. Cap."

Cap nodded at Jamila.

"Mr. Cap, what is on the other side of the door where you threw the body?"

"Go take a look."

Lorenzo looked at Jamila as she walked to the door and opened it up. She saw six hogs eating the body that Cap threw down there to them. Jamila closed the door back.

"Cap, I was told you had a brother named *1440*. Where is he? I would also like to speak with him."

"He is taking care of some business out of town right now. He'll be back in the next few weeks."

"When he comes back, let him know I would like to speak with him."

"I will let him know."

"Before we leave, Cap, there is one more thing. I don't want you to show up at none of my places of business. That's why I said I need you to be my shadow."

"I understand, Ms. LaCross."

"Good. Come on, Lorenzo, let's go."

Cap watched as they both walked out the shed and back to the limo.

Chapter Eleven

Slim Boogie opened his eyes to see Symone standing over him holding his hand.

"How you feeling, Slim? The doctor told me you've been waking up and going back to sleep. He had you in an induced coma."

"How long have I been here for?"

"Six months. You almost died on me. I've been coming by every other week to see you, but you've been sleeping every time I've come by. Today is the first day that you've been awake."

"I remember waking up from time to time. I would eat a little something or I would get a sponge bath, but I would go right back to sleep."

"Do you remember what happened? Why you are here?"

"I just remember running and getting shot at."

"You've had three blood transfusions and four surgeries. The doctors didn't think you was gonna make it, but look at you—the doctors say that you are at sixty-five percent right now. When you get to one hundred percent, I'll be back for you."

"So what's been happening out there since I been in here?"

"Red Invee is home, and we have mob ties with the Scott family and the Teliono family. Don't worry about nothing, Slim. Just stay here and heal up. I need you back out here with me. So, the sooner you heal the better it will be for us." Symone got up and kissed Slim on the forehead.

"Look, Slim, I have to go but I'll be back soon."

"I'll be here waiting."

Symone kissed Slim one more time on the forehead before walking out the door.

Slim closed his eyes and leaned his head back, knowing he needed to heal up because Symone needed him out there with her. Iceman walked Symone out the hospital to her limo that was waiting on her. He opened the door for her to get in.

"How is Slim doing?"

"Good. I talked to him for the first time today. Iceman, hold on, my phone is going off.

"Hello."

"Hello, Rose, how are you doing?"

"I'm doing good. How are you doing, Oso?"

"I'm doing good, Symone. I'm calling to let you know that this will be the last shipment I'm sending to you."

"I don't understand. Why is that?"

"Because we've hit a bump in our relationship, and I can't continue to supply you and deal with Red Invee. I understand that you have a lot going on between the two of you, but I have strong ties with Red Invee, and out of respect for her, I'm cutting ties with you. But we have been doing good business, so out of respect for you, I'm doubling your last shipment that I send you and then all deals are off between us."

Symone made a tight fist and had her head leaning against it as she had the phone to her ear, listening to Oso. She took a deep breath.

"You know what, Oso? I really, really respect that. Thank you. So when should I expect my last shipment?"

"I'm sending it out Sunday, right before I come up there to see Red Invee."

"OK. Thank you. I'll have the money wired to you within forty-eight hours."

"I'll let you know when I receive it, Rose."

"I'll talk to you then." Symone hung up with the look of death in her eyes.

"Is everything okay, Rose?"

Symone held her finger up to Iceman, signing for him to hold on as she called Halo.

"Hello."

"Halo, I just got a call from Oso telling me he's cutting us off because of the relationship he has with Red Invee. But, he did agree to double our last shipment."

"What the fuck! Are you for real?"

"Yeah, but I'm not worried about him. I have another connect that nobody knows about. But I don't know what the fuck Oso think. Don't nobody cut me off like ain't talking about shit. He said he's coming up here Sunday. I want him killed when he comes up here. He will not leave New York City alive. When his body goes back down to Mexico, it will be a cadaver, nothing else."

"I'll put a team on it, Rose."

"Halo, we have one shot, and I don't wanna fuck it up because I don't know how they will come back at us or who he will send. So we got one shot, one kill."

"I'm on it, Rose, trust me."

"I do. I'm on my way back to you now." Symone hung up and looked at Iceman.

"Iceman, a war is coming towards us. I need you to be ready because it's coming hard."

"I'm ready for whatever comes our way, Rose."

Chapter Twelve

"Hello, welcome to Panache Fine Jewelry. My name is Halo. May I help you with something?"

"Yes. I'm looking for a gift for my wife."

"Well then, you came to the right place. What do you have in mind?"

"Well, sir, I have a spending limit of one thousand five-hundred dollars."

"Well, that's just fine. Let me just walk you over to the show-case. I never got your name, sir."

"My name is Timothy Green."

"Well, Mr. Green, these are some of our best earrings and chains."

"May I see those diamond earrings right there?"

"Yes. You're talking about the red ruby earrings with the yellow diamond center. We call it the 'Sunflower' because you see how the red rubies look like leaves of a flower, and the yellow diamonds are the center. This is a very good choice."

"How much are the set of earrings?"

"One thousand two hundred dollars."

"That's in my price range. I'll take them. This is a very nice jewelry store, Mr. Halo."

"Thank you. Presentation is everything to us."

"Mr. Halo, I remember a few months back—this jewelry store had a different name."

"Yes. It was called Cody's Jewelry. We bought them out for a fair price. Well, Mr. Green, here is your wife's gift and receipt, and thank you for shopping with us."

"No. Thank you very much."

As Green was walking out the door, he stopped and looked back at Halo.

"Hey, question. Do you own the other Panache Fine Jewelry Stores as well?"

"Yes, we do. Feel free to shop at anyone of our locations in the city."

"You know what? I think I'll do that next time."

Halo watched as he walked out the door. There was something about him he did not like at all. Halo waited till Green was out the door, and then went and looked at the security cameras. He watched Green get into a black Ford Taurus, then he paused the camera and wrote his license number down.

***

"Lorenzo, how long before the new guy starts doing pick-ups?"

"I don't know, Tasha. When me and Red Invee went to see him the other night, he wasn't there. Just his brother, and that was a scary sight."

"What do you mean *scary sight*, Lorenzo?"

"When we walked around the side of the house, he had someone in there tied to a wooden X, doing nasty things to him. I mean he was doing some fucked up shit. I was just hoping that he'd put the gun to his head and kill that motherfucker. I looked at Red Invee and she was just watching. She never took her eyes off of him. In a funny way I think she was enjoying it."

Tasha looked at Lorenzo.

"Do you remember that day that Symone gave my son that bullet? I was so afraid for his life. The only thing I could think of was, killing her. I know she was somewhere watching the whole thing. I moved my family out of my house that same day. But I know she enjoyed watching me panic. I wanted to kill her so bad."

"Tasha, trust me, don't worry. Her time is coming."

Tasha stopped at the red light on 125th Street.

"Lorenzo, the city is big. You might not see Symone for another year."

Lorenzo looked past Tasha to the car on the other side of them, one car away from them.

"You gotta be fucking kidding me."

"What is it, Lorenzo?" Tasha asked.

"You see that white Lexus one car down?"

"Yeah."

"That's Lola. That's the bitch that set me up for Symone when they shot me up."

"Are you sure, Lorenzo?"

"Yeah. I am."

Tasha looked at Lorenzo as she pulled her gun out.

"Tasha, wait, not here."

"Fuck that, Lorenzo, we gonna get that bitch at the red light."

Tasha opened up her car door and ran to the back of the car. Lorenzo jumped in the driver's seat of Tasha's car. Tasha was ducking behind the other cars as she ran up to Lola's car, gun in her hand. She snatched Lola's car door open. Lola looked at her as Tasha had the gun aimed at her face. Shock appeared in Lola's eyes as she looked at Tasha.

"Lorenzo said I should deliver this message—'*Payback is a bitch*.'"

Before Lola could blink, Tasha started letting off round after round into her chest. All one heard was the sound of gunshots as Tasha emptied the clip into Lola. There were people jumping out of their cars and running. Tasha looked at Lola's lifeless body before she took off running. Lorenzo pulled the car up, and Tasha jumped into the passenger seat as Lorenzo took off driving.

"Lorenzo, that's how you kill a bitch. You catch them at the light."

"Are you sure she's dead?"

"If that bitch is still alive, she had the whole armor of God on her ass. *Tic tac! Pow!* I laid that bitch down. On God."

SAYNOMORE

Chapter Thirteen

"I know, I know, I see it on the news now. Rose just walked in. I'm telling her now. I'll call you back, Perk-G." Halo hung up as he looked at Rose. Rose took her jacket off and hung it on the back of a chair.

"What do you have to tell me, Halo?"

Halo shook his head, looking for the right words to say.

"Lola never got a chance to pick up that work from Perk-G today."

Symone took a seat at her desk, and put her hand on her chin as she looked at Halo.

"And why is that?"

"She got killed at 125th today at the red light."

Symone stood up. "What! Are you sure?" She pulled out her phone and called Lola.

"Rose, it's all over the news." Halo cut the TV on so Symone could see for herself. She placed her phone on the desk, as she watched Lola's car on the news.

"Word got back to me it was Lorenzo and Tasha that caught her slipping."

"Halo, have someone go and claim her body. Have Man and B.R. come see me now, both of them. Lola will not die alone today."

"Rose, it's hot right now, plus there is something else I have to talk to you about."

"Halo, one of our family members was gunned down at a fucking traffic light in cold blood. I don't give a fuck how hot it is Somebody gotta die."

"Rose I'm with you hundred percent but hear me out first. I had a visitor today. A detective came by posing as a customer and he was asking questions. I think we are being watched right now. I had a friend run his plates and it came back as Detective Timothy Green."

"Halo, we need to find a way out of this triangle. We are at war with the LaCross Family. Oso just cut us off of our supply of heroin.

Halo, we will not fall. Find out where this detective lives. We need to send him a message."

"I already got the address."

"Good. Have Pistol put the work in for me. I just want him to deliver a message, that's all. He can't afford to kill cops right now. Have Man and B.R. put some work in too. I need a body for a body. I'll take care of Oso with Iceman. I just need you to take care of everything for me right now. But right now, we need to knock the biggest threat off, and that's this Detective Timothy Green you were telling me about."

"Do you want him to take a swim in the Hudson?"

"No. I just want him to get a very clear message. Have Pistol write on his walls in blood, *'Walk away from this case, Detective Timothy Green'*."

"I'm going to take care of that right now, Rose." Symone took a seat behind her desk, as Halo walked out of her office. She promised herself, as she lit her Black and Mild, that whoever killed Lola was gonna have a horrible death.

Chapter Fourteen

As the story about Lola was being broadcast on the news, Jamila sat behind her desk, watching the news, drinking a cup of coffee. Lorenzo and Tasha walked into her office just then.

"Lorenzo, I see you caught up with her. You would think she would at least change cars. Tasha, I'm glad you put in the work for the family, but you need to be more careful because people are recording things these days and you don't need to be on the news killing people. Lorenzo, what did you do with the car? Tasha, you need to lay low. I know Symone is gonna come for you. She's gonna want a body for a body. It's how I taught her. She's gonna send somebody within forty-eight to seventy-two hours to get it done. So, make sure everyone is on high alert. Tasha, I want you at the restaurant with me. Lorenzo, Oso is coming next week to see me, so make sure the waste plant is clean and ready for the next shipment to come in. I want that place like a fortress."

"Let me go take care of that now, Jamila."

"Tasha, I want you on the floor. You are taking Lorenzo's place when he is not here."

"OK. I'm going to walk the floor now."

Jamila watched as Tasha walked out of her office, then she turned her attention back to the news.

***

Pistol looked at the time on his watch. It read 9:20 p.m. He opened his car door and walked across the street to Detective Timothy Green's house. He looked in the window downstairs; it was pitch-black in the house. He took two steps back from the house, noticing a light had come on upstairs. He walked to the backyard fence and saw a dog house where a dog was sleeping on a chain. He pulled out his black 9mm, put the silencer on it and aimed it at the sleeping dog, shooting the dog two times in the head. The dog died on the spot. Pistol hopped the fence and walked up to the dead dog. He pulled his knife out of his pocket and kneeled down over the dead dog. He looked around before he went to work. By 10:30 p.m. Pistol was done.

"Baby, wake up, you smell that?"

"Yeah, I do. Are you cooking something?"

"No, I'm not. I've been in the bed with you all this time."

Detective Green got up and pulled his gun out of his nightstand.

"Baby, stay here, don't move. I'm going to go check on the children."

With his gun in his hand, Detective Green walked down to his children's room. They were still sleeping in bed. He looked back at his wife, who was in the doorway watching him. He pointed downstairs at his wife. Step by step, he walked downstairs with his gun in his hand. When he walked into the kitchen, he saw that the stove was on with a covered pot boiling on top. He looked around the kitchen, but didn't see anybody. He removed the lid off the pot, and his dog's head floated to the top. His eyes popped out of his head. Detective Green jumped back and threw up on the floor. He looked at his sliding door to the backyard and saw a message written in blood on the glass.

The message read: *Walk away from the case detective Timothy Green. This will be your only warning.* He walked to his sliding door and opened it. He looked in his backyard, but didn't see anybody. He walked back to his kitchen, picked up the phone and called Chief Tadem.

Detective Green was fully dressed, sitting on his front steps, when Chief Tadem pulled up. Chief Tadem walked up to Detective Green, and looked down at him as he was sitting on his steps.

"So, tell me, Detective Green, what is so important that you got me out of my bed at twelve a.m. on the other side of town?"

"I had a visitor tonight. Go take a look inside." When Chief Tadem walked in the kitchen, he saw the dog's head still floating in the pot on the stove. Then Detective Green showed him the message written on the sliding glass doors.

"Fuck, Green, I told you this might happen. Where are your wife and children now?"

"I sent them to go stay with her sister for the week until I get this under control."

"This is why I didn't want you to open this case at all. I went through something like this about eight years back myself. Look, Green, just walk away from this case. Trust me, you don't want to play with these people."

"Chief, I just can't walk away from this case. They came in my fucking house."

"You're right they did come in your house, and it could have been your son or your daughter's head in that fucking pot. They came in my house many years back and I'm still alive, Green. I said the same thing to Detective Boatman, and look at the outcome. I don't wanna see you in a coffin by playing with these people. That's how it always ends up."

Chief Tadem pulled out his cigar and lit it.

"Look, I'm not gonna call this in. I don't need this getting out. I'm gonna let you clean up this mess. But just know, Green, these people have no problem killing a cop, and I don't want to open the paper and see your face on it. Green, just walk away from it. That's all I'm asking you to do."

"Chief, I can tell you I am, but I'm really not gonna walk away. They came in my house. It's personal now."

Chief Tadem looked at Green.

"Alright, have it your way." He turned around and walked off.

Detective Green yelled at him as he was walking off.

"So that's it! You don't have nothing else to say! That's it, sir! You're just gonna walk off like that!"

Chief Tadem got to his car, turned around and looked at Green.

"I'm not just walking off. I'll pay my respects at your services and say something nice about you."

Chief Tadem got in his car and drove off. Detective Green looked one last time before walking into his house.

SAYNOMORE

Chapter Fifteen

"Excuse me, Judge Keys, you have a Mr. Jones here to see you."

"OK. Stacy, bring him to the backyard," Judge Keys said over her walkie talkie. Judge Keys sat on his bench in his backyard by the lake as he fed the ducks pieces of bread. Mr. Jones and Stacy walked into the backyard as Judge Keys was feeding the ducks.

"Judge Keys, how are you doing today?" Mr. Jones asked him.

"Yesterday, today, and tomorrow, nothing's going to change. I'll be feeling the same way. What can I do for you, Jones?"

"A bird sung a song in my ear telling me that Jamila LaCross is at war with Symone Rose, Judge."

Judge Keys never turned to look at Jones. He continued to feed his ducks.

"Jamila is in Queens, Symone is in Brooklyn. As far as I know, Symone Rose is protected in Brooklyn. As of last week, Symone became a made lady. Jones, I don't think this is gonna be an easy win for Jamila LaCross because I know for a fact, Jones, that Symone has the Teliono Family and the Scott Family backing her up."

"I heard that the Scott Family and the Teliono Family is backing her up, Judge, but don't forget—Jamila still has the other four families' support. The Deniro Family, the Landon Family, the Lenacci Family, and don't forget the Gambinos. Not only that, history will prove that Jamila LaCross never lost a war. Do I have to remind you that she killed Jatavious Stone, Kent Washington, Felipe Conway, Mayor Oakland, Tony Lenacci, and Detective Moore? Do I need to go on, Judge Keys?"

"See, that's the thing, Jones, everyone you named let their position of power get to them as if they were untouchable and couldn't get killed. Symone knows her sister very well and how her sister moves. She knows when to cross the line. Like I said before, she is a made lady. No harm will come to her on those streets. So, tell me, Jones, what is it you came here to tell me besides Jamila LaCross and Symone Rose's war?"

"I just came by to tell you what I heard, Judge Keys."

"Now that you've told me what I already knew, Mr. Jones, I believe our conversation is over."

"I guess you are right, Judge. You have a good day."

"Likewise, Mr. Jones." Judge Key finished feeding his ducks as Mr. Jones walked off without looking back at him. He knew there was more to the reason why Jones came to see him. He wanted to know whose side the Judge would be on in the war to come.

Chapter Sixteen

Detective Green sat at his desk and was thinking about how someone was in his house. They could have killed his wife and children, and all Chief Tadem could say was: *walk away*. Detective Green couldn't help but remember the look of horror on his wife's face and the frightened look in her eyes, knowing someone had been in their house and had killed their family dog by cutting his head off and putting it in a pot of boiling water. She kept crying and saying: "That could have been one of our children." Detective Green was glaring at a picture of Symone hanging on the wall, when Detective Hall walked into his office.

"Hey, Green. I bought you a cup of coffee and a doughnut. May I have a word with you?"

"Yeah, come in and have a seat."

"Chief Tadem told me what happened last night."

"So I guess you're here to throw it in my face and say: I *told you so!*"

"No, I'm not. Look, I know how you feel. Trust me, I do. That's why I don't take on no cases involving the Mafia. Because we don't know who is on their payroll. Just like we keep in touch with other police departments to help us out on cases, they do the same thing in the shadows with other Mafia families. So we don't know who is telling them what. Green, this is a game that no one really wants to play, because you really can't win. I know you really don't want to hear this, Green, but trust me when I say this—*if you keep playing with fire, you're gonna get burned*."

"Hall, she had someone in my house. They cut my damned dog's head off and cooked it in a damned pot."

"That was the warning she gave you, Green. That same person could have killed you and your family. Your house could have been blown up. You could be dead right now." Detective Hall got up and looked at Detective Green. "Walk away. That's the last time I'm gonna tell you that."

Green watched as Hall walked out his office. Chief Tadem saw Detective Hall and called him to his office. Chief Tadem was sitting behind his desk, as Hall walked through the door of his office.

"Close the door and have a seat, Hall. I'm going to get right to the point, Hall. It's only a matter of time before Green gets himself killed. Maybe even his family. So, I'm pulling him off the case and putting you on it. And I don't need to say what I need you to do, right?"

"Chief, I ain't no boy scout. I know what needs to be done."

"That's all I need to hear then."

"Is that all, Chief Tadem?"

"That's all, detective."

Detective Hall got up and walked out of Chief Tadem's office.

***

Symone walked into the casino and went upstairs to her office. She sat down behind her desk, picked up the phone and called Iceman.

"Hello, Ms. Rose."

"Iceman, where are you?"

"Downstairs, at the casino."

"Is everything OK down there?"

"I'm trying to find out now."

"You know what? I'm on my way down there now."

After hanging up, Symone walked out of her office and went downstairs to the basement. Iceman had Lee Gambino tied to a chair, punching him in the face with his brass knuckles over and over again. Lee had blood all over his face.

"I'm gonna ask you this again, who had you come into my casino and try to pay off my workers?"

Lee looked at Iceman and started laughing in his face as blood came out of his mouth. Symone walked through the door as Lee was laughing.

She looked at Iceman.

"Who is he?"

"Lee Gambino. He came in here a few hours ago asking questions about you. One of the table workers overheard him, took a fifteen-minute break and came and got me. I asked him why was he concerned about you, and he brushed me off. I tased him, and here we are. Symone walked up and looked at him.

"Iceman, he's not gonna talk. Look at him. He's loyal to Chris Gambino. Kill him and send his head back to Chris Gambino. No, send his head to Red Invee."

"Do you think I give a fuck if you kill me? I knew I was dead when I opened my eyes and I was tied to this chair. I ain't no fuckin' rat."

Symone looked at him and pulled her gun out.

"And that's why I'm gonna kill you with respect."

Iceman and J. Mitch looked at her. Lee closed his eyes as she fired two shots to his head, killing him.

"Get his head to Red Invee and dump his body off somewhere. I'm going back upstairs and go over the numbers for this week. Call me if you need me."

SAYNOMORE

Chapter Seventeen

Jamila walked into her office to see Chief Tadem and D.A. Mack there waiting for her.

"Chief Tadem, D.A. Mack," she said as she walked up to them and shook their hands.

"I'm sorry I'm late, but Lorenzo told me just a little while ago that you two were here. So, tell me, gentlemen, what can I do for you? Wait, before you answer that, can I get you something to drink? Water, wine, or something a little stronger?"

"No, thank you—We are good," answered Chief Tadem.

"OK. So, how may I help you?"

"Jamila, we know about the differences that your family is having with the Rose Family, and we came to see how we can end this before it turns into a very chaotic war. In the last war we had, police officers were killed. Symone Rose does not care about or value life, and she will do whatever she has to get her point across. We witnessed that during your incarceration, when she was the head of your family. She is like a wild dog that cannot be controlled. D.A. Mack and I have elections coming up, and we cannot afford to look bad in the eyes of the public. The newspapers are already saying we cannot control our streets." Chief Tadem's face had a serious look.

Jamila didn't say anything. She just looked at him as he talked.

"What do you have to say, Mr. Mack?"

"Chief Tadem is making a point. We can't have chaos on top of chaos this time of year. It wouldn't look good for neither of us. We are asking if you could tone it down just a little bit until the elections."

Jamila got up, walked to her closet and came back out a few minutes later. She placed two envelopes on the table in front of Chief Tadem and D.A. Mack.

"I understand both of your concerns, gentlemen, and I'll do what I can to tone it down on my end. There's fifty thousand dollars in cash in each envelope I placed in front of you. I greatly appreciate both of you coming to talk to me today. Again, I'll do what I can on my end."

Jamila stopped talking when she heard a knock on her office door. She looked as Tasha walked in.

"I'm sorry to bother you, Ms. LaCross, but this package just came for you a few seconds ago."

Chief Tadem and D.A. Mack looked at the box Tasha had in her hand, as she walked and placed it on Jamila's desk in front of her.

"Thank you, Tasha."

"You're welcome, Ms. LaCross."

Jamila watched as she walked back out of her office.

"Chief Tadem and D.A. Mack, I will do everything to the best of my ability to keep things cool till after the elections. Now, if you two would like to stay for lunch it will be on the house."

Chief Tadem looked at Jamila.

"Thank you, Ms. LaCross, we would like that."

Jamila got up and shook both their hands.

"D.A. Mack, it was nice seeing you again."

"Likewise, Ms. LaCross, and thank you for the free lunch."

"You are very welcome."

Jamila watched as they walked out of her office. Once the door was closed, she opened the box that Tasha put on her desk. She took a deep breath and closed her eyes when she saw Lee Gambino's head in the box. She closed the box back up and walked to her bar. She poured herself a drink and called Mr. Chris Gambino. After two rings, he picked up the phone.

"Hello, Mr. Gambino."

"Ms. LaCross."

"We need to talk, Mr. Gambino. Are you gonna be at the fight tonight?"

"Yes, I am."

"OK. I'll see you there."

Jamila hung up and walked back to her desk.

Chapter Eighteen

It was 8:00 p.m. when Halo and Perk-G walked into the arena to see the UFC fight.

"You sure you want to make this bet, Perk-G?"

"I got ten thousand dollars. I know for a fact that cracker ain't about to lose."

"If you really think that a street fighter is about to beat a trained seven-year veteran Octagon fighter, you're crazy as fuck Perk-G."

"You know what? Just cash me out at the end of the fight, Halo. You know I want that free money."

"Well, I'm not going to talk about it anymore. We gonna see who will be cashing out who at the end of the fight."

"Say less, Halo. We could have watched the fight on Pay-per-view. Why did you want to come see the fight?"

"Because Rose said Lola's murder won't go unanswered. She wants blood for blood and a body for a body. And where do a lot of these big-time mafia motherfuckers like to come? Boxing matches and UFC fights."

"So whose bottle we gonna pop tonight?"

"Nobody. Our seats are over here to the right. Come on."

"So if we ain't gonna body a motherfucker or kidnap somebody, what are we here for tonight besides to watch the fight?"

Halo pointed his finger at the front row where Jamila was talking with Chris Gambino.

"That's why we are here. Nobody knows you, and nobody knows me. That's why we are all the way up here. To blend in with the nobody's. So just pay attention to who she talks to and who they are with tonight.

***

"I'm glad you could make it, Red Invee."

"Thank you for the invitation, Mr. Gambino. I'm sorry about Lee. He was a good man and very loyal."

"He was a very honorable man. I loved him like he was my own son."

"Mr. Gambino, I promise you he will not die alone."

"I take your word, Red Invee. I know he will not die alone. So, to my understanding, Rose has the Scott and Teliono Families backing her up now?"

"That is a true statement. She does have them backing her up now. But, I have a new shadow who can't wait to meet her new friends."

Mr. Gambino looked at Jamila and smiled.

"A shadow, you say?"

"That's what I said. And Rose is not a problem. She can't leave out of Brooklyn, and we control all of the other boroughs; so where is she gonna go?"

"You know what, Red Invee? You are doing the same thing Sammy and Alex did."

"And what is that, Mr. Gambino?"

"It means that you are understanding Rose. She is not as shallow as we would like to think. My sources tell me she has two judges, one D.A. and a few cops in Brooklyn now. Not only that. She made a new ally with the Teliono Family, and Teliono owns the docks. She is taking baby steps, but they are working for her, as you can see. She is getting just as powerful as you were coming up. It's getting to the point where she doesn't have to get her hands dirty anymore. She has workers and friends who adore her in other families."

"Mr. Gambino, I understand everything you are saying, but just like everyone else who went up against me, she will be killed too. As of right now I'm not going to react to anything. The elections are coming up, and Chief Tadem and D.A. Mack are running. So I need the streets to be calm until these elections are over."

"How do you expect to do that when Rose is sending you heads in boxes? I don't think this is gonna be a war that's gonna blow over. I do believe you have your work cut out for you this time."

"Mr. Gambino, I'll figure it all out."

"So, should I expect my drop to come this week, Red Invee?"

"Yes, everything will be ready for you this week. Everything is at a hundred percent, Mr. Gambino. So, tell me, who did you bet on?"

"The guy wearing the red and black shorts. He's hungry. He'll take his opponent down before the end of the second round."

Jamila nodded as she watched the fight.

SAYNOMORE

Chapter Nineteen

Halo walked into the casino and stopped when he saw Iceman talking to a man at the bar. Iceman looked up and saw Halo standing there. Halo tilted his head, giving Iceman the signal to come over to him.

"Mr. Clay, please enjoy the rest of your night. I have some business to attend to."

"Thank you for your hospitality, Mr. Iceman. I hope to see you again before the night is over."

"We will see, Mr. Clay."

Iceman patted him on the back two times before walking away.

"Halo, what brings you by?"

"I have a message from Rose."

"OK. What news do you have from the boss?"

"We are all going to meet on the docks tomorrow night at eight p.m. Rose got word that there's gonna be a drop there from Oso, and Jamila is gonna be present. So it's gonna be a night of fireworks like the fourth of July. Iceman, I don't know what she got planned, but she wants me, you, Perk-G, Man, B.R., J. Mitch, and Real Right there."

"Then there's nothing else to be talked about. The boss has spoken."

"Indeed. So, tell me, Iceman, what's been going on around here?"

"Everything you see, Halo—money, gambling, and women. The American Dream."

"Well, Iceman, I have to get back to the jewelry store. So be ready when you get the phone call, Iceman."

***

Jamila sat in her limo as the rain drops hit the roof while the limo pulled under the bridge. She looked out the window to see car lights coming under the bridge where she was meeting D.A. Jones.

She looked at him when he stepped out of his car. Masi opened the limo door, got out and stepped in front of D.A. Jones.

"Please lift your arms up so that I can pat you down."

"Sure, no problem."

Jamila watched as Masi patted D.A. Jones down before he got in the limo.

"Ms. LaCross, thank you for seeing me at a last-minute request."

"No problem. So, tell me, what was so urgent you had to see me tonight?"

"You told me to let you know when I hear anything of importance. I went to see Judge Keys a few days ago because I heard about the sparks firing between you and the Rose Family. So I went to talk to him about it, and he brushed me off. In so many words he said that it would be Rose standing over your dead body, that you would not win this war. He further said she's in Brooklyn, she's a made lady now, and she's protected."

"So you're telling me that Judge Keys is betting on me to lose?"

"That is the picture he painted when I was there. He didn't even want to talk about it. I don't know what plans he has up his sleeves, but I want you to watch out for him. I didn't want to talk over the phone just in case he had a tap put on my phone or yours."

"D.A. Jones, I really appreciate your loyalty to me. It's a shame I really did like Judge Keys. But don't worry about Judge Keys. He's old, and I've heard he is very sick now. So his day just might be coming soon."

D.A. Jones looked at Jamila one more time before opening the limo door and stepping out. Masi got back in the limo and closed the door. Jamila placed her hand on his knee.

"Masi, I need you to go see Young Cap for me. Tell him I said *Judge Keys*. Let him know the judge lives right off Avon, and that I want this one to be bloody and very loud. I want Judge Keys to know that this came from me before he dies, and that Brooklyn can't protect Symone from my wrath.

***

Vinnie stood at the end of the dock, smoking his Cuban cigar, waiting for Joe Scott and Chris Gambino to show up. He looked at the sea, thinking to himself how many bodies he'd had dumped in there. He turned around when he heard a car pulling up. When he looked, he saw two cars pulling up. He watched as both cars came to a stop, then their bodyguards got out and opened the doors for Joe Scott and Chris Gambino to step out. He watched as both men approached him at the end of the dock.

"Joe, Chris, I'm glad you two were able to make it here today."

"How are you doing today, Vinnie?" said Chris.

"I have no complaints. I'm doing fine."

"I'm glad to hear that. So, tell us, why me and Joe had to come out here to meet you?"

"I wanted to make sure nobody was following you two, and that nobody could see us having this meeting today. Rose is getting too powerful, too strong. Just like Red Invee did when she was coming up. And we know that you, Joe, sided with Rose against Red Invee—The Queen Don."

"Vinnie, I did side with Rose, and Red Invee is not my Queen Don."

"My question to you, Joe, is, how can you side with a female who killed more men in your family than anyone over the last twenty years?"

"Vinnie, wait, didn't you help Red Invee kill Alex to be where you're standing now?"

"Joe, I did what I had to do before Alex sent them all to the fucking graveyard with Tony."

Chris waded in quickly to kill the brewing tension between Joe and Vinnie. "Look, Vinnie and Joe, both of you need to cool down. Joe, all Vinnie is saying is: this could end badly for all of us. We've all known each other for years."

"Vinnie," said Joe, "just like you had to do what was best for your family, so did I, and if you asked me out here to talk to me about going against Rose, I'm telling you now, she has my loyalty, and you've just wasted my time and yours."

Vinnie smirked. "Joe, I'm trying to get you to see the big picture. You can't win. Rose can't win. Rose has shown us that already by every war that she's been in. I don't want you to force my hand. Because if I have to apply force in my own way, your name will go in the newspaper as deceased."

"Vinnie, I have floated more bodies in this river than you ever have, so don't force my hand. Now, if you two don't mind, I have things I need to do."

Vinnie and Chris watched Joe walk back to his car.

"Chris, like it or not—he needs to die. Walter Zimmerman knows Joe very well, and he'll convince Zimmerman to side with them against the Queen Don. So, we need to stop this now before Rose becomes any more powerful. I already got word that she's got D.A.'s, judges, and cops in Brooklyn. So, she's making Brooklyn her Queendom. What makes her even more dangerous is that everyone that's sided with her knows our weaknesses. They know who we do business with, so we need to end this fast."

"It's not gonna be as easy as turning a light switch on or off, Vinnie, but I do agree with you. So, let's get this done."

Vinnie shook Chris' hand, and patted him on the back before they walked back to their cars.

***

Young Cap looked around to make sure nobody was watching him as he picked the lock to the door. He opened the door very quietly and entered the house. He was looking at the pictures of Judge Keys and his wife on the wall. There were also pictures of his son hanging on the wall that Young Cap paid close attention to. When he looked at his watch, it was 4:30 p.m. He walked into the kitchen, looked out the window and saw Judge Keys sitting on his bench by the lake. The man was feeding his ducks, just like Young Cap was told Judge Keys would be doing. He stopped looking at the judge when he heard someone coming down the stairs. He put his back against the wall and pulled out his gun. He waited as the footsteps got closer and closer. When he looked down, he saw a shadow. He turned quickly and put the gun to someone's head. "Fuck up and die," said Young Cap.

"Don't scream. Don't even breathe hard. I'll rip your tongue out of your mouth. Don't fucking try me. Is there anyone else in this house?"

He watched as Judge Keys' wife shook her head by way of saying, *No*. Young Cap sat her down, pulled out a roll of duct tape, and taped her to the chair. Then he put a piece of tape over her mouth. He watched as Judge Keys got up and walked back to the house. He pulled the chair that Judge Keys' wife was taped to into the middle of the kitchen floor, so that Judge Keys could see her when he opens the back door. He went and stood behind the door with his gun in his hand. When the door opened, the look on Judge Keys' face was a look of horror when he saw his wife tied to a chair. When he looked around, he saw Young Cap. Before he could say a word, Young Cap smacked him on the side of the head with the gun, knocking him out cold.

SAYNOMORE

Chapter Twenty

Jamila watched as Oso's plane landed. She stood next to the limo between Lorenzo and Dro. They waited for Oso and his men to get off the plane. Oso smiled when he saw Jamila. He lit his cigar as he walked towards them. Jamila met Oso halfway, and they embraced each other with a hug and a kiss on the cheek.

"Jamila, it's good to see you. Has your shipment already arrived?"

"Yes. It should be in route to the waste plant now. I have a private limo so that you and I can talk privately on the way to the restaurant. Our men can follow us there."

Oso opened the limo door and let Jamila get in first.

"So, Jamila, tell me, what is it that you want to talk to me about?"

"Since Symone and the Telionos have become allies, I don't feel comfortable with my shipment going to the docks anymore. That's why I invited you up here. We need to figure out a new shipment route so my supply won't get delayed at all. For me to keep a hold on the city, I have to be able to supply the city. If I can't feed my city, then I can't rule over my city. A queen who can't feed her people is not a queen at all." Oso didn't say a word; he just nodded.

"Jamila, we have different routes, but you are the Queen Don. There are very convincing ways to show the Teliono Family not to touch, and our supply will still go through the docks. A man will find favoritism in you as the queen when he is in chains and L.K. walks up to him with a rubber apron on and gloves. You do remember the passion that L.K. has for the love of his job?"

"Yes, I do. How can I forget? Oso, we will discuss this topic more over dinner. I have a meal being prepared for us at the restaurant, and I know after your long flight you could use something to eat."

***

Judge Keys sat tied to a chair with nothing on but a pair of boxers. His wife was standing up, and she had nothing on. Her hands were tied to a pair of chains that hung from the ceiling. She was standing in a rubber swimming pool with water inside of it. She had duct tape over her mouth as she looked at Young Cap while he stood at a table with knives and a rubber apron on. Her eyes were puffy and red from crying. She had peed on herself twice already, knowing she was gonna die. The look in Young Cap's eyes told her it was going to be a horrible death. Young Cap looked at Judge Keys, picked up a bucket of ice water and threw it on him.

"Wake up. It's play time, Judge Keys."

Judge Keys was in a state of shock when the ice water hit his body.

"Who the fuck are you? What the fuck do you want?"

"I'm a shadow, and you'll only see me when it's time. And I only want your life."

Young Cap looked at Judge Keys as he walked over to him. He whispered in Judge Keys' ear.

"Ms. LaCross heard everything you had to say about her. So now, I'm her messenger to you." Young Cap moved away from Judge Keys and looked at Mrs. Keys.

"Let me start with you," he said.

Mrs. Keys looked at her husband, and with her eyes she was begging him to help her.

"Don't worry, Mrs. Keys, this might hurt and this might not. It all depends on how well you take pain." Young Cap placed a long sharp knife on Mrs. Keys' neck and ran it down her body, across her breasts to her stomach. He looked back at Judge Keys with a grin on his face as he dug the knife in her flesh. She was screaming through the tape with tears coming from her eyes, running down her face, shaking from the pain.

"Stop it, you sick fucker! Leave her alone! It's me you want! I swear I'll kill you for this. I swear I will!"

Young Cap didn't pay any attention to the threats Judge Keys was yelling at him. He walked and put two cables in the water. He walked back to the table afterwards, looked at Judge Keys and then flipped the switch. Instantly, a series of sparks seized the pool, sending Mrs. Keys' body into spasms, causing her to twitch and jerk until her eyes rolled to the back of her head. A horrid smell filled the air. That was when it dawned on Young Cap that Mrs. Keys had released her bowels.

"Stop it, please stop it!" Judge Keys cried to Young Cap. Young Cap laughed as he flipped the switch off. Mrs. Keys' body hung limp, dead. Young Cap walked up to her body with a knife and slit her throat from ear to ear. Judge Keys had just watched the woman he had been married to for forty years tortured and killed in a horrible way.

"Judge Keys, I'm not going to kill you the way I killed your wife."

"I swear I will kill you for this!"

"How are you going to kill me when you are a few seconds away from death yourself?"

"I'll kill you in the next life!"

"Maybe you will, maybe you won't." Young Cap put the 9mm to Judge Key's head, pulling the trigger and killing him instantly. He then shot him five more times in the chest.

"I'll see you in the next life, Judge Keys, and everyone else I killed."

***

"Jamila, this meal is to die for. It is very delicious."

"I will let the chef know what you said, Oso. So, tell me, what other way can we get my shipments to me, and where do the shipments need to go besides the docks?"

"We can fly it in, but the cost is gonna be much higher because the risks are greater on both sides. What we need to do is, get an overstanding with Mr. Teliono because we pay for the use of the docks, Ms. LaCross."

"I understand that, Oso, but a few weeks ago Symone became allies with the Teliono Family, and I just don't trust it at all."

"Red Invee, sometimes you have to trust blind situations no matter how big the risks."

"Oso, how much more will it cost me to have my product flown in?"

"The insurance will be one million, and there will be a new pick-up location."

"And where would this pick-up location be?"

"I will have to make a few calls and find out where and what would be the best time, day, and location."

"When will you be able to provide this information?"

"Let me make a few calls and get back to you in a few days. Red Invee, you do know I killed my brother, don't you?"

"No, I didn't know that."

"Well, I did. Sometimes you have to spill your own blood. Red Invee, blood don't make you family, loyalty makes you family. Blood makes you related. In my culture a mother will kill her son, and a father will kill his daughter. I have known you for many years now, Red Invee. I have witnessed you build your empire from the ground. Don't let this pebble that's in your path knock down your Queendom. If a mother could kill her son and a father could kill his daughter, then a sister can kill her sibling."

Jamila picked up her glass of wine and took a sip as she looked at Oso.

"How did Symone take it when you told her you were cutting all ties with her?"

"She was upset, but she did not let her emotions show. She said she understood and respected my decision. Do I trust her word? No. I've been in this line of work too long to take her word of respect and understanding. She took it too easy, but I might be wrong." Oso picked up his napkin and wiped his mouth with it.

"Red Invee, thank you for the meal. I'll be here until tomorrow night. I will stop by and see you before I leave."

"So where are you headed now, Oso?"

"I have another appointment that I must attend to." Oso got up and gave Red Invee a kiss on the left cheek, and a light hug before he and his men left the restaurant. Jamila walked to the front door.

Before going back to her office, she watched as Oso and his men drove off.

SAYNOMORE

Chapter Twenty-One

Halo looked out the window as he waited for Symone to come into the office. Word got back to him that Oso was in the city, and was staying at the Hilton, downtown Manhattan. Jamila convinced Oso to cut Symone off. Now they had to cut Jamila off, and the only way to do that was to kill Oso. Halo turned around when he heard the door opening up. He saw Symone walking into the office.

"Halo, you called me up here to tell me something good?" Symone walked to her desk and took a seat.

"Word got back to me that Oso is in the city, and he's staying at the Hilton in downtown Manhattan."

"I wonder why he's staying at the Hilton and not *Destiny's*," Symone stated. "But you know what, Halo? It doesn't matter. I want his fat Mexican ass dead before he can get back on a plane. We don't know how long of a window we have so send the shooters now. Halo, *bang*, *bang*."

"I'm on it now, Rose." Halo looked at Symone one more time before walking out of the door. Symone pulled a Black and Mild out of her purse and lit it. Then she picked up the phone and called Pistol. After two rings, he picked up the phone.

"Pistol, come by Panache. We need to talk." Without saying another word, she hung up the phone.

***

"Masi, what do we have here?"

"A fuck up, Lorenzo. There's only forty-five thousand from the two bricks we gave him last week."

"I didn't give him shit, you did. That's your boy, Masi." Lorenzo paused and scowled at Kane. "And *you* standing there ain't saying shit, but you eighty-five thousand dollars short, or you got that work put in the back somewhere? Don't look at the ground, motherfucker, look me in the eyes. Now, answer the question!"

"No. There's nothing in the back."

"So where the fuck is the money or work at?"

Kane looked at Masi.

"I don't know why the fuck you looking at him, 'cause if I tell him to bury your ass, he's gonna put you six feet deep with a hole in your head. Now you need to start talking, nigga."

"I was trying to open a new spot a few blocks from here, and on my way there I got ran down by the police and had to throw the bag."

"So when were you gonna tell us that, Kane?"

"I was trying to get the money up first."

"You had the right plan in mind. I'm giving you two weeks to get the money up or next time I see you its rock-a-bye-baby. You get the point?"

"Yeah, I get the point, Lorenzo."

"Good. Now go get Red Invee's money." Lorenzo watched Kane as he walked off.

"Masi, you brought him to the table. In two weeks if he don't have the money, you're gonna kill him and bring me back head proof. Your homie, your problem." Lorenzo looked at Masi one more time before going to his car. Masi turned around and followed him to his car.

Chapter Twenty-Two

Lorenzo walked into Jamila's office to see her watching the news, drinking a cup of coffee and eating a doughnut.

"Good morning, Jamila."

"It is a good morning. How are you feeling, Lorenzo?"

"I have no complaints. So, what's on the news this morning?" Jamila smiled and took a sip of her coffee. Lorenzo watched as she placed her coffee back on her desk.

"It's a sad story. Somebody killed Judge Keys and his wife. They tortured his wife before she died. It's a shame what happened to them." Lorenzo looked at Jamila. He knew she had her hands in their murder somehow, but he didn't say anything to her about it because he knew never to question anything she did. He just rolled with it.

"Yeah, that is fucked up, damn. I had Masi go with me when I pulled up on Kane about that money yesterday."

"Tell me, Lorenzo, what did Kane have to say?"

"He was trying to make a move down the block when the police ran down on him and he had to throw the pack."

Jamila looked at Lorenzo as she ate her doughnut. She put her doughnut down and wiped her mouth. "And you believed him, Lorenzo? Lorenzo, you know I have a yatch in the desert sitting on the ocean." Jamila stood up.

"Lorenzo, we're talking about two kilos of cocaine. Nobody is gonna throw that. And why would the police run down on him? Lorenzo, baby, he lied to your face and took from me. He failed. Have Masi kill him. Deadline—forty-eight hours. Nobody is gonna steal from me and live to talk about it. And I want everyone around him killed. Birds of a feather die together. And it won't be hard because wherever Kane is, so are my two kilos. As a matter of fact, find out where he is and take me to him."

"I'll get on that now, Red Invee." Lorenzo walked out of the office. Jamila picked up her doughnut and finished eating it as she watched the news on Judge Keys' assassination.

***

Oso went to his room door when he heard a knock at the door. His two bodyguards outside his room door were knocking to let him know that the limo was downstairs waiting for him.

"Mr. Oso the limo is downstairs waiting for you, sir."

"Good. I am so ready to leave New York. Grab my bags. They are over there on the floor."

Oso was looking at his phone, as he was walking down the hallway of the hotel. He had four men guarding him, two in front and two in back. Pistol was in the front lobby next to the swinging doors to the bar. He watched as Oso stepped off the elevator with his men. He picked up his phone and made a call as they went to the front desk to check-out.

"Iceman, be on point. There are four of them with him checking out."

"OK. He has two men out here next to his limo. Pistol, everyone is ready out here."

"Let's get this over with then, Iceman." Pistol hung up the phone, and watched as they made their way to the front doors. Pistol pulled his gun out. "Oso!"

Oso stopped to see who had called him. That's when he saw Pistol's gun aimed at him. "Oh shit, down, down!" one of Oso's men yelled. That's when Pistol started shooting at Oso. Oso's men pulled their guns and started shooting back, as one of his men grabbed him and ran to the front door. Pistol shot one of the bodyguards in the face while trying to shoot Oso. Bullets were flying back and forth. Pistol was shooting from the side of the wall, ducked down. Oso made it out front. Blood splattered everywhere as Iceman shot one of his bodyguards in the neck as he tried to get Oso to the limo. Oso watched his guard hit the ground. Oso bent down, picked up the fallen bodyguard's gun, and started shooting at Iceman.

"You want to kill me? Then come get my blood, Putos." Oso turned around to see two of his men shot down by Pistol. Pistol didn't see L.K. as he came up behind him and shot him three times in the back, dropping him. L.K. ran to the front doors to help Oso. As L.K ran through the hotel doors, he was shot twice in the side. The shots killed him right away. Oso ran to help him, but it was too late. Oso looked and saw one of the good guys running to the driver side of the limo. The back door was open, and all of his men were dead outside. He ran to the back of the limo. Once inside, before he closed the door, he yelled without looking: "Drive, drive!" He closed the door to the limo as it drove off. Oso turned around and was looking at Symone face to face. She was pointing a black 9mm at him.

"Symone, this is how you repay me? I helped you take over Brooklyn, I supplied you. I took you in as a friend, now you losing one."

"Oso, there's no such thing as losing a friend. You only lose enemies that you thought was your friend."

"So you're switching up on me now, like you did Red Invee? What happened to that word *loyalty* you stood on?"

"Oso, I never switched up on nobody. It's either you pushed me away or you forced my hand and—Oso, you and Red Invee forced my hand. You two underestimated me because I'm young. Trust me, I know more than I say. I think more than I speak, and I observe more than you know, and now our conversation is over. Symone pulled the trigger twice, and blood hit the back window of the limo. After Symone killed Oso, she looked at his dead body. She picked up her phone when she heard it ring.

"Hello, are you OK?"

"Yes. How is everything, Halo?"

"We're good. Pistol took three shots to the back but he's OK. He had his vest on. We got him out of there. The whole New York City Police department is down there right now, with two local news teams. Where's Oso?"

"Dead. Right here in front of me. Have everyone meet back at Panache."

"OK. I see you in a few."

Symone hung up and tapped the front window. Real Right rolled the window down.

"Yes, Ms. Rose?"

"Drop me off at Panache, dump the body in the Hudson, and have the limo chopped up."

"Yes, Ms. Rose.

***

Lorenzo ran into Jamila's office and grabbed the remote to the TV. Jamila was on the phone. She looked at Lorenzo like he was crazy.

"Let me call you back, Mr. Gambino."

Jamila hung up the phone, got up, walked over to the TV and stood next to Lorenzo.

"What's going on, Lorenzo? Why is that look on your face?"

"There was a big shoot-out at the hotel Oso was staying at not even forty-five minutes ago. Six people dead—all Hispanics."

"You got to be fucking kidding me. Don't tell me that, Lorenzo."

"Jamila, shit went *boom* today. It's a fucking mess right now. Jamila, this has Symone's name written all over it." Jamila didn't say anything. She was listening to the news reporter talk.

"*I'm standing here with Ms. Flowers at the Hilton downtown Manhattan. Ms. Flowers, can you tell me what happened here today?*"

"*It was a blood bath out here today. All you could hear was gunshots. I was standing right over there reading a brochure, when I heard someone yell: "Oh, no." I don't why, but when I turned around, a black man was pointing a gun at me. Then I heard two gunshots.*"

"*I see you have blood on your shirt, Ms. Flowers.*"

"*Yes. There was a man standing next to me, and he got shot in the head. Blood flew all over me, some got on my face. It was like being in a movie. I saw another man get shot down right there.*" *Ms. Flowers was pointing at the swinging doors where Pistol had been standing. Then the guy who shot him—I saw him get shot over there at those doors. In fifty-six summers I've lived, I've never seen anything like it before."*

"OK. Thank you, Ms. Flowers, for your time. As you can see, it looks as if an action movie was filmed here. There are reported six dead men, and one escaped in a limo. There is no word on the man who fled in the limo. The New York City police are still searching for the man who fled and the limo. We are told he was a heavy-set Hispanic man. Keep your station tuned here for more updates on the shootings in downtown Manhattan at the Hilton today. This is Channel Five action news in your home."

"I can't believe this shit. She just crossed the fucking line. The storm that is about to come her way is gonna make 911 look like a gang shooting. She just played with fire and got burned."

"Jamila, Symone is out of control. She acts like she's just fucking untouchable. This not only is gonna come back on her. It's gonna come back on us because he came to see you simply because you invited him up here. You know how that looks. Now we're involved in that bullshit."

"Lorenzo, we don't know if he's dead or alive yet, and I'm praying that Symone's shooters missed. Right now, what we need to do is find out if he's dead or alive. Everything else stops, because we don't know if it is Symone who has Oso's blood on her hands."

"Jamila, I know that's your sister and you could have killed her when you were locked up for her disloyalty. Fuck making excuses for her! You have to admit when she fucks up, and she fucked up big this time. It's time for you to chop her head off. It's either gonna be her or us because when Oso's people send their team, there's gonna be no understanding. It's gonna be a fucking replay of *Scarface*, and I ain't trying to have my brains on a globe of the world because your sister feels like she can do what the fuck she wants."

"Lorenzo, that is my fucking sister, and I pulled her into this lifestyle. You are right, but I will be damned if I'll let her get beat and tortured by those 'spic motherfuckers. I'll put a bullet in her head first. That is still my family, my father's child. Now, what you need to do is: beat your feet and find out if Oso is dead or alive, and come back and let me know."

Lorenzo just looked at Jamila.

"Lorenzo, why are you still here? Bye! And don't worry—we don't have a globe of the world here, so you don't have to worry about your brains being put on it."

Lorenzo walked out the door. Jamila turned around, walked to the bar and poured herself a drink. She took a shot of Hennessy. She turned around when she heard the news reporter. *"This is Barbara Smith of Channel 5 action news in your home. This is a live coverage of New York City Police department as they pull the body of a heavy-set Hispanic male out of the Hudson River. What we're being told is that the cause of death was two gunshot wounds to the head."*

"Fuck, Symone! Fuck!" Jamila picked up the bottle of Hennessy and threw it at the office wall, breaking the bottle.

Chapter Twenty-Three

Symone was smoking a Black and Mild, watching the news in her office with Halo.

"Symone, do you realize that you are becoming a threat in New York City?"

"Good. I'm not to be fucked with. When I flip the coin, motherfuckers die. I'm good in Brooklyn, and Brooklyn is my Queendom, and my knights are pulling up."

Symone stopped talking when her office door opened up. Iceman, Real Right, Pistol, Perk-G, Man, and B.R. walked in with J. Mitch behind them. Symone stood up and clapped her hands.

"That's what the fuck I'm talking about. When we pull up, we ain't doing no talking. We want all the smoke. We got Brooklyn on lock. We poppin' bottles, and motherfuckers respect the Rose Family. That fat fuck cut us off and got put on the grocery list. Now he's sleeping with the fishes. We ain't bending. We ain't breaking. We ain't folding. Perk-G, we have twice as much work as before. I want everything bricked up. Man, B.R. and J. Mitch, I'm breaking you three up. Man, you gonna be at Panache with Halo and me. B.R., you gonna be with Pistol at the House of Diamonds. J. Mitch, you will be with Iceman at the casino. Real Right, I want you with Perk-G. Perk-G, how long will this last shipment last us?"

"Three, to four months, or maybe a little longer, Rose."

"Good. That gives me enough time to find a new connect. And I already had one in mind. Halo, do you have something you wanna bring to the table?"

"Yes, I do, Rose. Listen, y'all, Jamila already know that Symone pushed the button, but she won't come to Brooklyn. Well, she don't have to. She's well respected, and she's got shooters that will come. Masi is one of her shooters, and he's crazy enough to pull up in Brooklyn on the fuck shit. Lorenzo has a lot of friends, so watch who you talking around, 'cause the same motherfuckers that will smile in your face is the same motherfuckers that will have you on a meat hook. That's all I got to say, Rose." Symone looked around at everyone.

"Loyalty—trust—is our foundation. Don't ever let anyone rip us apart. Shoot or get shot."

"The Rose Family above any other!" everyone said together.

Chapter Twenty-Four

"Chief, how are you just gone take me off the case, knowing how important this case is to me!"

"Look, Green, I gave you a shot, and it came back to you and your family. Your family could have been killed! I'm not gonna have your blood on my hands. That's just out of the question. It's over, detective. The case is no longer yours!"

"This is some bullshit, and you know it, Chief. It came back to me 'cause I don't make deals with criminals and I don't give them passes. I don't know how to turn the cheek like other officers of the law, Chief Tadem."

"Detective Green, you better learn your place before I drop your ass back down to traffic duty. I know you're upset, and you are a good detective, damn good, but don't let this case cause you to lose your family, job, or your life." Chief Tadem paused to let out a sigh.

"Now Green, I already gave the case to Hall. He wasn't happy about it, though. We already have the body of one of the biggest drug lords in a freezer downtown, with two holes in his head, and six of his men all dead. And from what I was told, the hit came from Symone Rose. The same person you were trying to build a case on. Think about this, Green. That could have been Emily, Jack, or Sarah on those ice trays downtown. You might not see it right now, but trust me—I'm doing you a favor right now."

Detective Green looked at Chief Tadem and walked to his office door. Before opening the door, he turned around and looked at him.

"You know, Chief, I'm glad my wife and kids weren't sitting in the house at gunpoint, like your family was, because that would have been the day I laid my badge down. That would have been the day when it would have become *kill or be killed*. Fuck my oath, fuck my pledge, fuck my honor and dignity, and fuck my badge and blue uniform."

Detective Green walked out the door after saying that.

***

Masi walked to the front door and knocked two times.

"Who is it?"

Masi didn't say anything. He heard the door being unlocked. When the door opened, he put his .45 caliber pistol in the man's face.

"Fuck up and die."

The man closed his eyes and put his hands in the air. Masi pushed the man back. At that point, Lorenzo and Dro walked into the house with two AR-15's in their hands. They went into the living room where Kane and his boys were playing NBA2K. They didn't see Lorenzo or Dro walk up behind them. That's when Jamila and Tasha came into the house with their guns in their hands. When Lorenzo saw Jamila, she nodded at him. Then she shot the TV out. Kane jumped up and turned around. He was in shock when he saw Jamila and Tasha with their guns pointed at him and his boys.

"See, this is how a motherfucker gets killed. You have music blasting, playing a damn video game. This motherfucker just opened the door, not knowing who was on the other side. Now here I am in your house with two AR-15's and a .45 caliber, and two 9mm pointed at you and your boys." Kane looked at Jamila and watched her talk. He didn't say anything.

"See, maybe you can help me out, Kane, but I need some clarification and understanding about some shit. But first, Masi, you and Dro bring his boys over there with him, and if any of them move, kill them. Bring their guns over to this table."

"Get the fuck over there, nigga, and try me if you want, nigga! I'm itching to kill a motherfucker," Masi said as he pushed Kane all the way on the floor.

"Y'all got the game fucked up if y'all didn't think we was gonna pull up," Dro said, as he got the guns off the table. After sitting Kane and his three boys down on the floor next to the wall, Jamila walked into the kitchen and saw one of her kilos on the table.

"Lorenzo, come here for a second. Let me show you something." Jamila walked back out the kitchen and looked at Kane on the floor.

"So, I see you got the kilos back, Kane. How'd you pull that one off?"

Lorenzo just looked at the kilo on the kitchen table. Lorenzo walked out of the kitchen and looked at Jamila.

"So, Lorenzo, I guess the officers decided to give them back their own property, their lost-and-found bag." Jamila looked down at the coffee table.

"Lorenzo, I see that we are sponsoring this party that they're having. Lines of coke on the table. Blunt in the ashtray. I'm shaking my fucking head. Masi, you brought Kane into my family, so you're on pause for one year, no recruiting, plus you have to pay the one hundred and twenty thousand dollars that Kane fucked up of mine. You brought him to the table, so he's your responsibility. Lorenzo, you let this man lie to you, to your face. That shows me he doesn't respect you, but don't worry. I'm gonna take care of this one."

Jamila went and whispered something into Tasha's ear. Tasha walked to the kitchen. Jamila walked up to all four of them on the floor with their hands tied behind their backs.

"So I'm gonna let you guys make the choice of whether you live or die. 'Cause in my eyes all of you are guilty for stealing my shit. Back in the 1600's, they would have cut your hand off for stealing, but I'm gonna try something different tonight." Jamila paused and cast a glance at Dro.

"Dro, get the one in the middle and take him to Tasha. If he try anything, kill him."

"Ms. LaCross, I swear I didn't have nothing to do with this. I swear on my children, I didn't."

"I don't wanna talk. The kitchen is that way." Jamila just looked at Kane on the floor.

After Dro brought Dee into the kitchen, Tasha put a gun to his head.

"Take your right hand and put it on the eye of the flame, and it's gonna stay there for two minutes, or there gonna be two bullets in your fucking head."

Dee looked at Dro and knew he would kill him with no questions.

"Put your hand on the fucking burner, nigga! You got three seconds and I'm gonna count from two."

Dee closed his eyes and put his hand on the red-hot eye of the stove.

"Ahhhh—ahhhh—ahhhh! Please let me take my hand off!" Dee cried.

"Shut the fuck up, chump, and you better not move that bitch," said Tasha.

"You have sixty seconds left," Dro said

Dee took a deep breath right before he passed out from the pain. Dro looked at him passed out on the floor. The flesh from Dee's right hand was melted beyond recognition from the fire. Jamila walked to the kitchen door and saw Dee passed out.

"Did he last his two minutes, Tasha?"

"No. He had thirty seconds left, Ms. LaCross."

"It's a shame. Dro, kill him Two gunshots echoed through the house as Dro killed Dee.

"Kane, that's one of your boys down. It's a shame. So, who's next? As a matter of fact, Masi, Lorenzo, kill all three of them. Dro, burn the house down."

"Wait, wait, wait!" Kane yelled.

Jamila turned around as Lorenzo and Masi let off round after round, killing them all. As she got in back seat of the Hummer, she looked back and saw Lorenzo, Masi, Dro, and Tasha come out of the house, while the house went up in flames. Tasha and Dro followed behind Jamila, Lorenzo, and Masi as they drove off.

"Masi, you do remember my rules, right?"

"Yes, I do, Ms. LaCross."

"Did you tell them to your friend?"

"Yes."

"So he should have known if he fucked up he was gonna die."

"He should have known. I did tell him."

"Masi, you have seventy-two hours to have my money. I'm not upset at you, but this is a lesson learned. You fucked up and it cost you a hundred and twenty thousand dollars."

"I understand, Ms. LaCross."

"Good. Lorenzo, take me home now."

SAYNOMORE

Chapter Twenty-Five

Symone walked through Marcy Projects in Brooklyn. She threw a fair for all of the residents. There were three trucks passing out groceries, school supplies for the kids and hot meals. She had over ten people working the grills, and ice cream carts for the children. There were rides for the kids, and prizes for the games that they won. All of the residents were outside with the music blasting, enjoying the carnival that Symone was putting on.

"Just look at her taking pictures with them, smiling and laughing. Kissing their children and passing out food. Who the fuck is she trying to fool?"

"Detective Green, look, Chief took you off this case. I'm only out here with you because we are friends, but don't make me choose my badge over our friendship."

"Mack, she had her men in my house. My wife don't feel safe there anymore."

"I don't know that feeling, Green, but I do understand how you feel, because I would want that bitch dead too. Just look at her. No matter how much blood she spills, they love her down there. No matter how many pictures you take of her, Green, it's all gonna be thrown out in court. No matter what evidence you get, it'll all get thrown out of court because we have no warrants for any of it."

"Don't worry about it. I know how to make it stick, Mack, trust me."

"I'm sure you do."

***

"Symone, this right here is crazy. We are in the open right now."

"Halo, trust me, we are good. There are too many people out here right now, plus I'm sure there are undercovers out here taking pictures and everything. No matter how bad Red Invee wants my blood, she's not stupid."

A tennis ball rolled and hit Symone on the foot. She bent down and picked it up.

"Here you go, little angel," said Symone.

"Thank you, Ms. Rose," answered a little girl

"No problem. Do you want some ice cream?"

The little girl nodded with a smile on her face. Symone took her hand and walked her to the ice cream cart.

"Which one do you want, Princess?"

"The one with Sponge Bob."

The ice cream man gave the little girl the ice cream.

"OK. Now, run back over there with your mother." Symone waved to the little girl's mother as she went back to her.

"Excuse me, Ms. Rose, may I have a second of your time, please?"

"Sure." Symone held up one finger, motioning for Halo to hold on.

"Hey. What can I do for you?"

"Ms. Rose, my name is Sandra. My son just graduated high school, and all he talks about is college. But I don't have the money to put him through school, and I don't have the heart to tell him that he can't go to college. All he talks about is school, Ms. Rose."

"Do you know which college he wants to go to?"

"He says LSU."

"So he wants to be a tiger?"

"Yes, he does."

"OK. Look, this is what I want you to do, Sandra. Do you know where Panache Fine Jewelry is in Brooklyn?"

"Yes, I know exactly where that is."

"Tomorrow at two p.m. you come and see me. You and your son."

"OK. Thank you, Ms. Rose."

"No problem. Make sure you are there."

"I promise I'll be there. Thank you again."

Halo watched as little kids ran up to Symone to say: "Thank you", and to give her hugs and kisses. The kids and their parents took pictures with Symone. Halo kept watching as people came to talk to her about their problems.

"What's going on, Halo? How long have y'all been out here?"

"I've been out here since twelve p.m. with her. She's been talking to people, playing games with kids and taking pictures with them. It's going on five hours I've been watching her, Pistol."

"Any sign of Jamila and her team."

"Not once have I seen any of them. It's been real peaceful out here today."

"That's good. How long does she plan on staying out here?"

"To tell you the truth, Pistol, I don't know. I've never seen this side of her before. I've never seen her smile this much before. By the way, where the fuck you been at all day?"

"I got a call from Slim Boogie. They discharged him today. I went and picked him up. He's at the house right now."

"Is he at one-hundred percent, Pistol?"

"As far as I could tell, he is. From the way he's talking, he's ready to get back in the streets, and push the button on anybody that's got a problem with Rose."

Symone turned around and saw Pistol. She walked over to him, and gave him a hug and a kiss on the cheek.

"What's up, Pistol? So, you decided to come to my block party."

"I was on my way earlier, but got a phone call from Slim Boogie. I had to go pick him up. I'm just now getting back."

"Where is he now?"

"Home, getting himself together."

***

"Green, do you have everything you need?"

"No, all I have is a bunch of pictures of her helping to feed the kids. By making plates for them, kissing the children, and playing games with them. She don't even have her men with her, except for that guy standing next to her. His name is Halo, and I don't know who the fuck this guy is that just pulled up on them, but I got pictures of his ass too."

"Green, Rose is not stupid. If you want to get to her, you've gotta have records. I mean shit that could incriminate her, things that can link her to crimes to show who she really is. All this shows is that she's a guardian angel for the less fortunate in Brooklyn. Find the records, get the files and you'll have a case against her. Just don't let it blow up in your face, and remember what you have at risk."

"I know what I have at risk, man, and I will nail this bitch to the cross. Come on, let's get out of here."

***

"Symone, we need to go. We have other business we need to see about, and check on Perk-G. Besides, I know you wanna see Slim Boogie."

"Yeah, you right, Halo. Let's go." As Symone was leaving, a little girl ran up to her.

"Ms. Rose, are you leaving now?"

"Yes, I have to go now, Princess. Don't look so sad, I'll be back."

"OK. Thank you for everything, Ms. Rose."

"You're welcome, Cutie." Symone knelt down and gave the little girl a hug and a kiss, and watched as she ran back to her mother. Symone waved to both of them before she turned to leave.

***

Jamila walked into her office to see Gino Sabrano sitting down. Lorenzo had already told her that Gino was in the office waiting for her. She had never met him before until today, but she had heard stories about him. He was an older white male in his late fifties. He was sitting next to her desk with both hands on top of his silver and gold cane. He was heavy-set, with black and gray hair, a clean-shaven face and a look of determination.

106

"Mr. Sabrano?"

"Yes. You must be Jamila LaCross?"

"Yes. I am."

Jamila walked over to him, and they shook hands as he stood up.

"Let me start by saying you have a nice establishment here."

"Thank you. May I ask the nature of your visit?"

"Yes. I've been getting reports of this ongoing war between you and Symone Rose. And the other families have been losing money because of this war. Now they are saying you took on the Lenacci Family, the Deniro Family, and the Scott Family and won. But, they don't feel that you are ready to kill your own sister. They're asking for the blood that she has spilled in their families."

"Mr. Sabrano, your name comes with a great deal of respect, and once upon a time you were in my position as the head don. I have worked very hard to keep things in line with all the families, Mr. Sabrano. I've given them more protection than they've ever had before. I've given them my all."

"They know and respect this, Jamila. They have no arguments at all to disagree with what you are telling me. It's like you said before, a mad dog must be put down if it cannot be controlled on a leash. Jamila, don't take this the wrong way but you are the first black female don. Times have changed, 'cause back in my day you would have been killed. You wouldn't have even been allowed to be a part of the mob. Your position is one of power and great responsibility. So this is what I bring to your table today, Ms. La-Cross. You are not allowed to go after Symone Rose. You are not allowed to step on her turf in Brooklyn. The other families will take care of her. Word already came to me that she is the one who killed Oso. Because of her actions, a lot of money the families are gonna lose, so you will stay in Queens and let the rest of the families take care of the Rose Family. If you step out of line and go after her, you will lose your current status as the head don. Remember: Nobody is bigger than the mob."

"So, you're telling me I can't do anything? I have to sit on my ass and let everybody else deal with her."

"It's the best thing for you, Jamila. The most dangerous person in the world is the one who listens, thinks, and observes. Sometimes, things are out of our hands, trust me. I've been in tight corners before, but what I've learned and how I made it this far is— sometimes it's best to let some things go. It's the right choice, no matter how you look at it.

"Mr. Sabrano, I thank you for your advice and your time. I will let the other families deal with her. But, I will say this, I trained her, so it won't be an easy victory for them. At all."

"There's never an easy victory at war, Jamila. You either win or you lose, that's it."

Jamila shook Mr. Sabrano's hand before he left her office. She took seat at her desk, thinking about what he said to her. She knew his power and position. Mr. Sabrano walked out of her office and made a call.

"Vinnie, this is Sabrano. You have the green light. I want to hear something in seventy-two hours." He hung up the phone as he got in his car.

Chapter Twenty-Six

Slim Boogie was in Panache Fine Jewelry with Halo.

"Yo, this place is fly as hell, Halo."

"Yeah, wait till you see the other four stores, and the casino, and strip club."

"Facts, where is Rose at?"

"Shit. Only God knows that answer, Boogie. Follow me to the back so that I can show you the new stuff that came in last week."

Halo stopped walking when he heard the front door open and the bells ringing. He turned around and saw two Italian men walking in. Slim, let me see to these customers that just came in, and I'll be right back."

"Hello, welcome to Panache. May I help you?"

"You sure can. Tell Rose she's shut down."

Halo looked at them as they pulled two guns out.

"Oh, shit!" Halo pulled his gun, but the two Italians had already started shooting. Halo tried to run but got hit in the right shoulder and flipped over the counter.

"Fuck! You are two dead guinea motherfuckers." Slim came from the backroom, shooting at the two Italians.

"Halo, you good?"

"Yeah, just kill them motherfucking guineas." Halo was ducking down behind the counters.

One of the Italian men addressed his co-shooter: "Come on, come on, Vinnie just wants her to get the message. Rose will get the point. Let's get the fuck out of here." Then the same man spat, while shooting at Slim and Halo where they were taking cover: "You niggas are shut down, do you hear me?"

Slim watched as they ran out the front door.

"Halo, get up. We got to get you to the hospital now."

"Fuck! Slim, go lock the front door and we're gonna go out the back."

***

Symone walked the main floor of the casino, talking to Alex Forester, an investor with D.E.O Corporations. She was showing him the layout, hoping this would open doors for future business opportunities. She stopped walking when her phone went off.

"Will you excuse me, Mr. Forester? I have to take this call. Hello?"

"Hey, this is Pistol. We got hit today, and Halo got shot."

"Where was the hit?"

"Panache. Slim said he heard one of the guys say: *Vinnie just wants her to get the message*."

"Where are you guys right now?"

"House of Diamonds."

"Stay there. I'm on my way now." Symone hung up and walked back to Mr. Forester.

"Mr. Forester, I'm sorry, but I have an important matter that I need to attend to. Please enjoy yourself. My staff will accommodate you on whatever you need."

"Thank you, Rose. I think I will try my luck at the blackjack table."

"I wish you the best of luck," Symone said as she walked off.

"J. Mitch, get my car. You coming with me. Iceman, they just hit Panache. Halo's been shot, and I'm on my way to see him now. Make sure you watch the front door. We don't know who's who."

***

Everyone looked when Symone walked into the House of Diamonds. She didn't say a word. She went straight upstairs and into Pistol's office to see Halo.

"Halo, what happened?"

Halo had his shoulder wrapped, and he was sitting in a chair, taking shallow breaths.

"Two guinea motherfuckers came into the shop. They caught us down bad. If it wasn't for Slim Boogie, I would have been dead."

"Slim, call everyone. If it's not the Teliono Family or the Scott Family, I want them dead. I want their restaurants shot up. I want

110

their night clubs shot up. I want their pool halls burned down. We hit everything, starting tonight. I want the Red Carpet burned to the ground. In flames!"

SAYNOMORE

112

Chapter Twenty-Seven

'The war in New York City ran across all the news stations of late. There's been news about the car bombings, shootouts, night clubs being set on fire, bodies being found in the Hudson River and in back allies, cars being shot up, police killings, funerals being shot up, people coming up missing, judges and D.A's bodies being found in abandoned buildings, kidnappings of wives and children whose bodies are being found in parks. New York City has become a war zone over the last few months.' Mr. Sabrano cut the T.V. off after watching that news cast. He turned around and looked at Big Bubba.

"The other families wanted to deal with Symone Rose. I gave them the green light. Every time I turn on the TV, I see bodies being found. Cops, D.A's and judges are being killed. Symone Rose is not gonna lay down, and it's too hot for me to go and see her right now."

"You know what, Sabrano? You need to set up a meeting with Jamila and Symone Rose. They need to talk face to face."

"And how do you suppose I do that, Bubba?"

"What's that nigger Reverend's name? The one who always tries to keep the peace? Have him do it, but you need to guarantee them both safety on both ends. That's the only way it's gonna work."

"You may be right. Pass me the phone. I'll make the call now."

***

"Jamila, you've made a big impact on the City of New York, but with the good always comes the bad. There have been more deaths in the last decade than I have seen in my whole life. Jamila, do you believe that you play a big part in God's plan for New York? You don't have to answer that question. Just think about it. See, it's easy to kill a man. The swing of a sword or a single bullet will do the job, but forgiveness comes from the heart. It takes strength to walk away and not let pride stand in your way. To be the bigger person and walk away is stronger than a blow to a man's face. The flock that stands behind you will follow your lead. See, I came here to see you today with the permission of Gino Sabrano. His wishes are that you and Symone Rose will end this war between the two of you by having a face-to-face meeting and come to an agreement. Will you agree to this meeting, Ms. LaCross?"

"Pastor Rose, you are right, there is a time for war and a time for peace. These are my terms for this meeting. I'll meet with her, just me, her, and our second-in-command and no one else, and we will have the meeting at the old lake cabin."

"I will let Mr. Sabrano know that you have agreed to the meeting and your terms. Now, if you'll excuse me, I have to go see Ms. Rose. Take care, Ms. LaCross."

"You as well, Pastor Rose."

***

"Ms. Rose, thanks for agreeing to meet with me today."

"Anytime, Pastor Rose."

"Ms. Rose, joy comes at the price of pain. Sometimes it's like the sun shower. It's raining one second, and then it's beautiful and the sun is shining in the next few minutes. I said that, to say this: You, Ms. Rose have the ability to bring the sun out if you agree to this meeting with Ms. LaCross, and stop the rainy days."

"Pastor, rain waters the earth, and brings forth new life and green pastures. It's like the pain is necessary for a better tomorrow. What benefit will I get out of meeting from my sister?"

"Symone, I ask out of a request, but Gino Sabrano is demanding this meeting."

Symone got up and looked out of the window.

"I'll have this meeting with my sister. Will Mr. Sabrano be attending the meeting?"

"Yes. As a neutral party for both sides, and he guarantees safety for both sides. The meeting will be at the old lake cabin at five p.m. tomorrow, and you are only allowed to bring one person to the meeting. Ms. Rose, let's stop the stormy weather and bring out the sun again."

"Thank you, Pastor, and I'll go there with an open heart."

"And that will be the best thing for everyone, Ms. Rose."

SAYNOMORE

Chapter Twenty-Eight

Jamila's limo rode down the bumpy road, headed to the lake cabin.

"How do you feel about this meeting with Symone?"

"Lorenzo, I haven't seen my sister in two and a half years. I don't know the thoughts that will come to my mind when I see her. I knew Mr. Sabrano was still in the picture, but it's been over eleven years, and for the first time ever he comes to see me, because of my little sister."

"Jamila, he respects you, and I hate to admit it, but things were getting out of control between the two of you. This war was five times worse than the war with you and the Lenacci Family. This war had everyone involved. You made your sister. She thinks like you, moves like you, acts like you. That's why she is so feared, because they don't know what to expect out of her. She's fearless. Look at how she took over Brooklyn at the age of twenty-eight."

Jamila didn't say anything. She just listened to Lorenzo talk. The limo came to a stop. She looked at Lorenzo.

"You are right. I did make her in my image, and sometimes, the owner has to kill the dog. No matter how well trained the dog is."

When Jamila's door opened, she stepped out and looked around. She saw Gino Sabrano and two of his men.

Jamila and Lorenzo walked over to them.

"Mr. Sabrano, it's good to see you again."

"Likewise, Queen Don."

"Mr. Sabrano, I believe you know Lorenzo, my second-in-command."

"Yes, I do remember him. I remember your father, Lorenzo. He was a good man. Jamila, it's time to end this war. Sometimes it's the hardest thing to do, but remember no one is bigger than the mob. You are the Queen Don, and the choice you make today will tell who you really are. There is no such thing as favoritism, and everyone is held accountable for their own actions. Sanctions and dues will be required from this meeting today. And I will voice my opinion today as well. Here she comes now, Ms. LaCross."

Symone's limo pulled up. Everyone watched as she got out the limo. She had on a white mink coat, a white Dolce and Gabbana shirt, with a pair of white leggings, and white stiletto Timberland boots. Her hair was in black and blonde kinky twists. She had a pair of Versace shades covering her eyes. She had two diamond earrings on, a matching watch, and a tennis bracelet. J. Mitch was right next to her as they walked over to everyone else. Jamila just looked at her sister. She hadn't seen her for two and a half years. She wasn't the little girl she once knew. Now she was a bossed-up bitch. Symone stopped and looked at Jamila standing there. Jamila was wearing a gray and black Chinchilla with a black shirt and a pair of gray jeans hugging her thighs, with two-inch black stiletto shoes on, her hair was pressed down the side of her face. For the first time in years, Symone felt intimidated looking at Jamila, knowing that she was nothing to play with. She didn't see her sister; she saw an executioner, and she knew right then and there that she was on trial at that meeting.

***

Detective Green broke into Panache after disabling the alarm system. He had his gun out as he looked into each room to make sure nobody was there. "OK. Ms. Rose, let's see what you got in your shop that you wanna hide from me." Walking up the stairs, Detective Green checked behind every painting he came across to make sure there wasn't a safe hidden behind it. Once in Symone's office, he found a filing cabinet, but there was nothing in it.

"Think, Green, think. There has to be something in here." Walking over to her desk, Green turned her computer on.

"Fuck! I should have known it would have a pass code on it."

As he turned off her computer, he heard noises coming from downstairs.

"Shit! Who the fuck can that be?"

Detective Green looked around and went into the bathroom inside of Symone's office. He heard two people talking as they walked into her office.

"Halo, where is Rose now?"

"She had a meeting with Red Invee and Gino Sabrano."

"Who went with her?"

"J. Mitch. Look, Slim, we need to pick up these twenty keys of heroin, and drop them off with Iceman and Pistol. I just needed to come by here first and pick up the keys to the stash truck. I don't know how I forgot them. Come on, Slim, we out."

"I'm right behind you, Halo."

Detective Green heard when they closed the office door. He looked out Symone's office window, and saw them leaving in a black BMW. He ran downstairs and out the back door to his gray Honda Accord to catch up with them.

***

"Ms. Rose, it's a pleasure to finally meet you."

"No, the pleasure is all mine, Mr. Sabrano."

"I can honestly say that your father Anthony Catwell's blood runs deep in the both of you." Symone was looking at Jamila, while Jamila was looking at Symone.

"Symone, I don't think you were taught the laws of the mob. Do you mind if I go over them with you?"

"No, please, I want to know what the laws are, Mr. Sabrano."

"First, before you can start a family, you have to get permission from the family that you were once a part of. Ms. LaCross, did you grant permission for Ms. Rose to start her own family?"

Jamila looked at Symone with an iced grill.

"No, I didn't grant Symone permission, Mr. Sabrano."

Symone just looked at Jamila.

"Ms. Rose, how did you become the Don over Brooklyn? Did somebody give you Brooklyn?"

"No, no one gave me Brooklyn, Mr. Sabrano. I took Brooklyn, with blood and force and open arms from the Scott Family."

"Rose, I can't take away what you have. Yes, you did take Brooklyn, and there's still blood on the streets from that war, but no one is bigger than the mob. We are not divided at all. There is only one Queen Don, and she is standing in front of you right now. I'm here as a witness to this meeting to ensure the safety of you two, and to make sure nobody violates the terms of this agreement. I will say this before stepping to the side. We cannot undo what you have accomplished. Brooklyn is yours, but there are rules and guidelines you will follow, and one question you need to answer that I must know.

"And what is that, Mr. Sabrano?"

"Did you order the assassination of Oso?"

Symone looked at Mr. Sabrano.

"Not only did I order the assassination, but I put two bullets in his head. I did that myself."

"Queen Don, she's all yours."

Jamila looked at Symone as she took two steps towards her. She took the dark shades off so that Symone could look into her eyes. Symone took off her shades too, so that she could look into Jamila's eyes, showing no sign of fear.

"Symone Rose, your family has to pay one point five million dollars in sanctions for Brooklyn, plus an additional one point five million dollars for breaking Mafia laws. Furthermore, you have to pay three hundred thousand dollars in back dues. Your family will become a part of the seven again. And don't get me misunderstood, I'm not asking you. I'm telling you. "

"I thought that as you being the Queen Don, there were no dues."

"As much blood as your family and the Scott Family spilled, you're lucky to even have a family. You are not allowed to do no drug deals outside of Brooklyn."

"Is that all, Ms. LaCross?"

"No, there's also a blood price."

Symone looked at Mr. Sabrano when Jamila said that. He flipped both of his palms open and shook his head at her. When Symone turned around and looked, Lorenzo already had his gun out and he shot J. Mitch in the head twice. Symone watched as his body dropped. Before Jamila could say a word, Symone had her gun pointed at her face.

"I should fucking kill you."

Lorenzo had his gun pointed at Symone as she said that.

"Give me a fucking reason, Rose," said Lorenzo.

"I gave you three the last time we saw each other, Lorenzo. To your chest."

Jamila walked up to Symone and put her own forehead to the barrel of Symone's gun.

"If you think I'm scared to die, you got me fucked up, Rose. I've killed more motherfuckers than you can imagine, so go ahead, little sister, pull the trigger."

Mr. Sabrano just stood watching, not saying anything.

"I'll make sure you have your blood money, Queen Don. I'll have it delivered to you."

Symone looked at her driver with her gun still pointed at Jamila.

"Put his body in the limo," she said to the driver. Then, looking back at Jamila, Symone said: "I'll follow the laws, but don't push me."

"No, don't push me, pup," Jamila said.

Symone looked at Mr. Sabrano.

"Nice meeting you, Mr. Sabrano."

"Likewise, Rose."

"I see you held up very nicely, Lorenzo, let's not have a repeat." Symone blew Lorenzo a kiss before walking back to her limo. Mr. Sabrano got up and walked to Jamila.

"I see now how she was able to take over Brooklyn. She's fearless, and she stands behind her family. Jamila, understand what I'm about to say. It's either gonna be you standing over her body, or she will be standing over your body. Next time she gets out of line, kill her."

Jamila looked at Mr. Sabrano, as he walked back to his limo. He looked back at Jamila.

"I hope I don't have to come back down here again, Queen Don."

She watched him as he got in his limo.

***

Green pulled out his cell phone and called Detective Hall. After two rings, he picked up.

"Hello?"

"Hall, it's Green. Listen, I'm following two of Rose's guys. They're on their on the way to pick up twenty kilos of heroin."

"Green, you gotta be fucking kidding me. Let the case go. You're not on it. Let the damn case go, plus, the chief closed the case two days ago. It's over with, Green, it's done."

"What the fuck you mean he *closed the case*?" Green looked at his phone and hung up. He pulled over to the side when he saw them get out of the car. He watched as they got into a black 4 x 4 pick-up truck. He followed them all the way to Perk-G's operation. He took pictures of them loading the truck, and the girls who were bringing them the bags. He followed them to both drop-off spots. He had pictures of Iceman and Pistol, as both of them gave up bags and took bags from both spots. Green made sure he wrote down the addresses and both license plate numbers to the car and truck.

"You done fucked up now, Rose. Symone Rose, you will have a football number and the rest of these fuckers with you. I promise you that."

Chapter Twenty-Nine

Symone opened the door to Panache. She looked around when she noticed the alarm system didn't go off. She pulled her gun out and walked around back.

"What the fuck! Somebody cut the alarm wires." She walked back inside and locked the back door. She went to her office and watched the video tapes from the previous day.

"You just don't learn, detective, you just don't fucking learn."

Symone picked up the phone to call Halo.

After a few rings, he picked up.

"Hello," answered Halo.

"I need you to come to Panache now, with Slim." She hung up after saying that. Twenty-five minutes later, Halo walked into Panache with Slim. Symone was still in her office, watching the video tapes of Detective Green, when Halo and Slim walked into her office.

"Both of you, have a seat. Halo, let me ask you something. Yesterday, when you came in here, did you notice anything strange?"

Halo looked at Slim then back at Symone.

"No, why?"

"What about you, Slim?"

"No, I didn't notice anything."

Symone got up.

"So neither one of you noticed that the alarm system was deactivated?"

Slim and Halo looked at each other.

"Let me show the two of you something while you were in here talking business yesterday. Guess who else was in here with the both of you."

Symone turned the monitor around and showed both of them Detective Green inside Panache, then inside her office hiding in the bathroom.

"But that's not the fucked-up shit at all. Look at what he does when you two walk out. He walks to my office window to see the

SAYNOMORE

car you are driving, then he runs out of my office. So you know what that tells me?"

Slim and Halo just looked at Symone.

"He followed you two. You led him to Perk-G, Iceman, and Pistol. Fuck! Both of you, come with me. We need to go see Iceman, Pistol and Perk-G before my spots get raided. Come the fuck on."

Both of them followed Symone as she walked out the door.

***

Perk-G looked out of the peephole before answering the door after he saw it was Symone.

"What's up, Rose? Is everything good?"

"Perk-G, I don't mean to be rude but I need to have a look at your video cameras now!" Perk glanced at Halo and Slim with a look of confusion.

"OK. It's right this way. Come on, Ms. Rose, here are the monitors."

"I want to see the hours from seven p.m. until ten p.m. last night."

Perk-G rewound the video back to what Rose wanted to see. Symone didn't say anything as she watched the security tapes.

"That's it. Pause the video tape, Perk. Halo, Slim Boogie, come look at this."

Perk-G was dumbfounded; he didn't know what was going on.

"You see this? The same fucking gray car from Panache you two brought to Perk-G's operation. You weren't even paying attention. Look at his car windshield. That's not a fucking telescope he's looking through. That's a fucking camera that he's using to take pictures of y'all. So we know that he now has pictures of everything you guys did last night, but we don't know if he recorded anything. You two stay here. Perk-G, liquidate everything. I want everything out of here now. Slim Boogie and Halo, you two had better not lose one fucking kilo. I have to reach out to Iceman and Pistol, because I need both of their places cleaned out as soon as possible. You two

124

have probably given New York's finest the keys to our front door, and that's not what the fuck we need right now."

"Rose, so what do you wanna do about Detective Green?"

"Nothing right now, Perk-G. We need to clean this place up before we have twenty FBI agents kicking in our door."

SAYNOMORE

Chapter Thirty

Jamila was watching the news as Styles brought her food to her. It had been three months since she had let him taste her, and she felt she needed his tongue, if not more, inside her again.

"Come here, Styles, after you put my food on the table."

Styles put the food on the table and made his way over to her.

"Yes, Ms. LaCross?"

"How have you been?"

"Good."

"I haven't seen you in a while. Have you been hiding from me?"

"No, I just didn't want to say the wrong thing to you again. I don't want you to feel I was being disrespectful."

"I respect that, Styles. Did you have a good time while you were up here with me?"

"Yes, I did."

"Good." Jamila got up and walked over to him.

"I'm glad you did, but I want to see how thick and long your manhood is. Take your pants off for me. Let me see what you have down below."

Jamila sat on the couch and watched as he lowered his pants.

"Take them off slow for me, baby boy."

Jamila licked her lips as he got undressed for her. She saw the imprint of his penis through his briefs when he pulled his pants down.

"Walk over to me, Styles."

When Styles walked over to her, she reached with both hands and pulled his briefs down in front of her face. She looked up at him with seductive eyes as she bit her bottom lip, as she looked at his thick, long penis. It had a curve at the tip of the neck. She had never seen someone that thick before.

"Take your shirt off for me. Let me see your chest." Jamila stood up in front of Styles while he took his shirt off. She grabbed his penis as she kissed his neck tenderly.

"I need you to fuck me nice and slow. Can you do that, Styles?"

"Yeah, I can. I got you, beautiful." Styles turned Jamila around, unbuttoned her pants, and pushed them down. He couldn't stop looking at Jamila's small waist, her fat butt, and thick thighs. He just looked at how her ass swallowed the red G-string she was wearing. Once Jamila's pants came off, she lay back on the couch, still holding on to Style's penis. He lay on top of her, taking her leg and placing it on his shoulder. Jamila let out a light moan as he put himself inside of her.

"Damn, you are a big dick ass nigga. You breaking my walls down, Papi."

"Your pussy is so wet, tight and warm."

Jamila pulled him closer to her and whispered in his ear.

"Whose name is this on your shoulder?"

"That's my girl's name."

Jamila pulled him down to her and bit his shoulder where his girl's name was tattooed. She placed her leg around his back as he took long deep strokes inside of her. She was digging her nails into his back, as he was kissing her forehead.

"Damn, baby, I'm about to cum all over this dick."

Styles turned her around and started hitting it doggy-style. As he was smacking her ass, he wrapped his arm around her waist, then went deeper and deeper into her. He looked down at his dick going in and out of her as she was creaming all over her pussy. He grabbed her very tight as he released his seed inside of her.

"Damn, baby, I feel that in my stomach."

Styles pulled out of her, taking deep breaths. Jamila looked at him as he lay down on the couch. She kissed his lips and lay down in his arms, and he held her tightly.

Chapter Thirty-One

Detective Green barged into Chief Tadem's office with two folders in his hand. Chief Tadem looked at Detective Green as he interrupted his conversation with FBI Senior Director Smith.

"My apologies, sir. I didn't know you had company."

"That's the point of knocking and waiting for a response. Then you open the door after the response, Detective Green. As you can see, I'm talking with Senior Director Smith of the FBI, so you are gonna have to excuse yourself and come back at another time, detective."

"No, Chief, it's quite alright. Look at the detective's determination. He rushes in here, and he has two folders in his hand." Senior Director Smith looked at Detective Green curiously. "What you got there, son?" he asked. "Here, take a seat next to me and let's see what you have there."

Chief Tadem looked at Detective Green as he sat next to Senior Director Smith.

"Here you go, sir."

Senior Director Smith opened the folders and looked at all of the pictures inside.

"Are these pictures of the notorious Symone Rose?"

"Yes, sir, and I also have recordings of people in her organization talking about pick-ups and drop offs with addresses."

"Who are these guys right here?" asked Senior Director Smith, pointing at Symone's men one after the other in the picture.

"That, I do believe, is her second-in-command—Halo. I don't know anything about the other guy, but I did hear Halo call him Slim Boogie."

"What do you mean you heard Halo call him Slim Boogie?" Senior Director Smith asked him.

Detective Green looked at Chief Tadem and then back at Senior Director Smith.

"Yesterday night around seven p.m. I broke into Panache, and I was looking around to see what I could come across to build up a case against Rose and her organization. That's when I heard someone come in, so I hid in the bathroom. I heard them talking about picking up twenty kilos of heroine. They came by to pick up the keys to the stash truck. After that, they stepped out of the jewelry store, and I took off after them. I took pictures of the car they were in, and the truck they used afterwards. And here are the pictures of them making the pick-ups and drop-offs.

"Detective Green, who are these girls in these pictures?"

"I don't know, Senior Director Smith, but I do know that the man with them is named Perk-G, and here are pictures of Iceman and Pistol. Iceman runs the casino for her, and Pistol runs the strip club for her."

"Detective, you took all of these pictures last night?"

"Yes, Senior Director Smith. And in this folder are pictures and videos I took of her three days ago, when she threw a fair for Marcy Projects in Brooklyn."

"Senior Director Smith, Detective Green was taken off of this case two weeks ago, and I had this case closed."

"Sir, I understand I was taken off of this case, but she had her goons in my house, not yours. They cut my dog's head off and cooked it while me, my wife and children were upstairs asleep. I can't just roll over and pretend that nothing ever happened."

"Chief, he has a point." Senior Director Smith placed both folders on Chief Tadem's desk.

"Chief, make the call and get the warrants. Come to think of it—if they were in my house, hell would freeze over, and I wouldn't handle the culprit with kid gloves and just act like shit ain't happen. Even if we don't get shit, we can have an open case on this bitch and her family."

Chief Tadem looked at Senior Director Smith and Detective Green, then picked up the phone and made the call.

"Thank you, Senior Director Smith," said Detective Green.

"No, thank me by locking this bitch up. Chief Tadem, I think it's in your best interest to put Detective Green back on this case and open it back up. We don't lie down or brush dirt under the rug. We put monsters in cages, and wild animals to sleep."

Chapter Thirty-Two

Symone's limo pulled up to the docks. Her driver got out, walked to the back of the limo and opened the back door for her. As Symone got out of the limo, she noticed a lot of activity going on at the docks. She saw forklift drivers putting cargo onto the backs of trucks that were coming right off the boats. She looked around and saw Glen Teliono talking with someone. She made her way towards them.

"So let me clarify this, Mr. Teliono, for the next three months everything is paid for, and there will be no problems with my ship-ments coming in?"

"That is correct, Mr. Bento. You are three months clear here. I will have my men load your trucks, and your men can take them wherever they need to go."

"Mr. Teliono, I appreciate your business."

"No, Mr. Bento. I appreciate you trusting me with your cargo ships and your merchandise."

"Your business comes with a great reference, Mr. Teliono."

Mr. Bento looked and saw Symone coming their way.

"I believe you have a visitor, Mr. Teliono, and—may I say— she is very beautiful."

"Let me introduce you, Mr. Bento."

Symone walked up to Glen Teliono, hugged him and gave him a kiss on the cheek.

"Symone Rose, allow me to introduce you to Anthony Bento."

"Hello Mr. Bento, it's nice to meet you."

"Likewise, Ms. Rose, I've heard so many stories about you. Now, I'm looking at you face to face, the beautiful Symone Rose— who strikes the fear in the toughest men in New York City."

"Mr. Bento, that is not true," Symone said as they both laughed.

"Well, it was nice meeting you, Ms. Rose. Mr. Teliono, I have to be going. Both of you, have a nice day."

"You too, Mr. Bento," Symone and Teliono chorused.

"Symone, so what brings you by?" asked Glen Teliono as he put his hand on Symone's lower back.

"I had a meeting two days ago with Jamila LaCross."

"You had a meeting with Jamila LaCross?"

"Yes, but not by choice. At the old lake cabin. A Pastor Rose came to see me and told me that a Mr. Gino Sabrano requested that I be there."

"Gino Sabrano was there?"

"Yes, he was. He was with two other men. I never got their names."

"He must have thought that this war was getting out of control for him to come down here, away from his house in the hills. So what did he have to say?"

"He asked me whether I was responsible for the assassination of Oso and his men, and he wanted me to know that there was only one Queen Don and that she was standing in front of me, and her name is Jamila LaCross. Then he passed the torch to Jamila so that she could ask me or say whatever she needed to ask or say to me. In so many words, she said we have to come back to *the Seven*, plus I was sanctioned fines and dues for breaking Mafia laws. I have to pay three million dollars. And additional three hundred thousand dollars."

"Rose, they can't stop you, so what they'll do now is try to break you. I witnessed when your sister Jamila came up. She took out a lot of heavy hitters. I've had the pleasure of watching you come up. You are more fearless, brutal, and dangerous than your sister ever was. They fear you. Look how you took over Brooklyn."

"I forgot to tell you Brooklyn is mine. Gino Sabrano said they can't take away nothing that I have accomplished. Then Red Invee said they needed their blood payment back, and then they killed one of my guys in front of me. There was nothing I could do. I was outnumbered and outgunned, but I did put my gun in Red Invee's face before I left and told her to walk on eggshells around me. Queen Don or not."

"I see. We will all come back to *the Seven*. One thing I will say is, we don't want to cross or piss off Mr. Gino Sabrano. Trust me, he has enough power and pull to have us all killed. I can assure you of that. And if he left you Brooklyn, then that means he likes you, Symone."

"Well, Mr. Teliono, I came by to let you know about my meeting a couple of days ago. Now I have to go meet with Mr. Scott."

"You don't have to go see Mr. Scott. I'll inform him of all the details you just told me about. Thank you for coming by, Symone Rose, and look at it this way—going back to *the Seven* might not be bad at all."

Symone nodded as she walked back to her limo.

***

Jamila looked at everyone sitting at the diamond table in her office.

"I called you all here because as of three days ago the war with Symone Rose ended. She is not allowed to do no business outside of Brooklyn. Furthermore, the Rose Family, the Teliono Family, and the Scott Family will all have to come back to *the Seven*. As far as Oso's assassination, yesterday I had an hour-long phone call with members of his cartel family, about the whole thing. In our eyes Oso was doing good business on the up and up, but down in Mexico he was cutting a lot of his business partners off, and people were disappearing with no cause or word of their whereabouts. This all happened after Morwell's death. All fingers were pointing at Oso. So, in the end they've all agreed to continue to do business with us, with no bad intentions towards the LaCross Family. I want to thank all of you for your loyalty to me and to one another. We are still the strongest Mafia Family in New York City, and it will stay that way. We earned our stripes with blood, sweat, and tears. We walked through hell and came out on the other side without getting burned." Jamila stopped talking, and everyone got quiet when her office door opened and Symone Rose was standing there with a briefcase in her hand. Symone looked like a real boss bitch as she walked into Jamila's office.

"Please, don't stop your meeting because of me, continue."

Jamila walked from her place at the table and stood face to face with Symone.

"What are you doing here?"

"What? You're not happy to see me?" Symone giggled as she sat the briefcase on the ground.

"Don't worry, Red Invee. I just came by to drop something off to you, Queen Don. Everything you asked for is in this briefcase, down to the last cent."

"Masi, come get this briefcase and pass it to Lorenzo for me," Jamila said, never taking her eyes off Symone.

"Here, I have another gift for you." Symone gave Jamila a white box that was gift-wrapped. Masi took that box as well from Symone and put it on Jamila's desk. Symone leaned in and kissed Jamila on the cheek, then took her thumb and wiped Jamila's cheek off where she kissed her. Everyone was looking at Symone.

"Dro, Masi, walk Ms. Rose out of my restaurant and to her car."

Dro got up and looked at Symone. Symone smiled before walking back to her limo, where she had Iceman and Pistol waiting for her. Jamila walked to her desk and picked up the box that Symone left her. She unwrapped it, and it was a statue of a black lady wearing a white suit and eating a hot dog. Some of the ketchup had spilled on her white shirt, and underneath the statue—in gold letters—was written in block letters: *ACCIDENTS HAPPEN*. Jamila smiled when she read it.

***

"So where are we headed now, Ms. Rose?"

"To Panache. I have some phone calls I need to make, Iceman." Symone looked at Iceman as his phone was going off. He looked at Symone before he answered it.

"Yeah? Wait, wait, slow down. Are they there now?"

Symone and Pistol looked at Iceman as he was talking on the phone.

"OK. OK. I'm on my way there now."

Symone looked at Iceman as he hung up.

"Iceman, what's going on?"

"The *Jump Out Squad* are raiding the casino right now."

"Fuck! I knew this was gonna happen. Is there anything in there?"

"No, nothing. I cleaned everything out."

Pistol's phone went off and he quickly answered it. Symone looked at him when he hung up the phone.

"They are raiding the strip club right now, but we cleaned it out too."

"I just knew this shit was gonna happen. I just hope that Perk-G shit is cleaned up as well. Somebody, call Perk and let him know what's going on, and that he needs to get out of there."

***

Perk-G walked out the back room, smoking a blunt when he heard his front door being kicked in. When he looked, he saw the *Jump Out Squad* running up in his brownstone.

"Don't fucking move! Hands in the air now!"

Perk-G put his hands in the air as they put cuffs on him. One of the officers snatched the blunt out of his mouth and threw it on the floor. All one heard as they ran in each of the rooms was: "Clear, clear, clear!" Perk-G walked outside and saw thirty officers as they put him in the back of a squad car. They didn't say anything as they drove him to the police station. They took him straight to the interrogation room.

"Have a seat right there, Mr. Walter Johnson. My name is Detective Hall, and this is Detective Green. We need to ask you some questions."

"I don't got shit to say to you."

"Well, you know what? Don't talk, just look at these pictures for me. Show him the pictures, Detective Green."

Perk-G leaned back in the chair as they showed him pictures of him giving Halo and Pistol the black duffle bags to put in the truck.

"What do you have to say about this, Mr. Johnson?"

"Not a damned thing. Now if you motherfuckers don't mind, I need my phone call." Just then, there was a knock on the interrogation room door. Detectives Green and Hall stepped out.

"Hey, guys, the place was clean. There was nothing in there but the blunt he was smoking. He had everything wiped down good."

"Fuck!" Detective Green said.

"Thanks, officer," Hall said to the dude who had called them outside the interrogation room.

"Green, give him his phone call. He's clean. We have to let him go."

"I know this, Hall, I know this." Green opened the door and looked at Perk-G.

"You must have a leprechaun up your ass. We're cutting you loose." Perk G smiled when they took the handcuffs off him.

Chapter Thirty-Three

Symone sat in her office, looking at her attorney as he went over the warrants with her.

"Mr. Williams, did they have proper jurisdiction to raid my establishments?"

"Yes, they did, but they got nothing out of them."

"So are they gonna back off me now?"

"Nine out of ten times, no. They might try to get you for tax evasion."

"I pay my damn taxes every year. I cover my tracks, Mr. Williams."

"I'm not saying that you don't, Ms. Rose, but you've just embarrassed New York City's finest. They raided three of your establishments and came out with nothing. How do you think that makes them look? Right now they don't have anything on you, so you need to walk lightly before we'll be having this conversation through a glass window."

"I have judges and D.A.'s that will throw my case out, Mr. Williams."

"You don't have federal judges or D.A.'s. This is bigger than Brooklyn. The next time it won't be New York City's finest kicking in your door. It will be the Federal Bureau of Investigation, and when they come, they will have everything they need to hide you. Ms. Rose, I have to get going but take my advice: *Walk lightly.* You are now under the microscope. Don't give them a reason because they only need one. Trust me." Mr. Williams got up and walked out of Symone's office after saying that. As Mr. Williams was walking out of Symone's office, Halo was coming into Symone's office.

"Halo, close the door and have a seat. We have a problem that I need to take care of."

"And what is that, Rose?"

"Perk-G called me and told me that we only have sixty kilos left. We are running low on heroine, and I need to find a new supplier."

"So what do you have in mind, Rose?"

"There is only one person who I can think of who will supply me with what I need."

"Who is that?"

"Felipe's brother. Diablo. I know he's got what I need and more, Halo."

"Ms. Rose, I've never questioned you, but isn't his brother the one who killed your father?"

"Yes, he is."

"Ms. Rose, I know you and your sister are having your differences right now, but if you cross those lines, she may never forgive you at all—because this goes deeper than your loyalty to her. I mean it also questions the loyalty to your father, and that would be unforgiveable. Sixty kilos should last us three months."

"You know what, Halo? Call Pastor Rose and tell him I'll be stopping by the Living House of God to talk to him on Sunday."

"I'll go do that now, Ms. Rose."

"Thank you, Halo." Symone watched as Halo left her office.

Chapter Thirty-Four

Detective Green knocked on Chief Tadem's door.

"Come in."

"You wanted to see me, sir?"

"Yeah, Detective Green, have a seat. I'm going to get directly to the point. So, you barge into my office while I was having a meeting with Senior Director Smith, with your two folders of pictures and recordings. You wanted to be back on the case, you got it. You wanted your warrants, you got them. Three thirty-man teams raided every spot you wanted, and what do we have to show for it? Not a damned thing. Do you know how many man hours have been wasted? How much money this cost the department! How embarrassing this is to us!"

"Sir, listen, I know how this may look, but trust me. I know what I saw."

"Trusting you cost the department money, man hours, and embarrassment. I'm dropping your rank, and you are suspended."

"Suspended for what, sir?"

"For going behind my back and taking it upon yourself to do a stakeout and investigation on Symone Rose. You are suspended for four weeks with pay."

"You gotta be fucking kidding me."

"Keep that attitude up, officer, and it will be without pay. You're lucky I have a soft spot for your wife and kids. When you return to duty, you will be back in blue uniform."

"Sir—"

"That will be all, officer."

"Chief—"

"I said: *that will be all, officer.*"

"This is some bullshit and you know it." Detective Green walked out of Chief Tadem's office and slammed the door behind him.

***

Symone walked into the Living House of God off 114th St. Pastor Rose was giving a sermon, as Symone sat in the back of the church. Two hours later when church was ended, Symone got up and walked to the pastor, clapping her hands. "Now Pastor Rose, that was a good sermon."

"I'm glad you were able to hear the word of God through me."

"I really needed to hear the word today, pastor. Anyway, Pastor Rose, I need to talk to you about another matter."

"Ms. Rose, what is this other matter you need to talk to me about?"

"I need you to get in touch with Gino Sabrano for me and let him know I wish to speak with him. Will you do that for me, Pastor Rose?"

"I will try to reach him, and I'll let you know something in the next two or three days, Ms. Rose."

"Thank you, Pastor Rose, and here's a little something for the collection plate."

"The church is grateful for your donation, Ms. Rose."

Symone nodded at the pastor and walked away.

"Ms. Rose what is your favorite book in the Holy Bible?"

"I like First Kings, because Jezebel was loyal to her husband and king no matter how you look at it. Also, I like the Book of Ruth because Ruth was loyal to her mother-in-law. In addition, I like the Book of Esther, because Esther showed patience and obedience to her uncle, and because of her resilience she saved her people."

Pastor Rose nodded at Symone. She turned around and walked away after she acknowledged him.

***

Symone stopped at the flower shop and picked up two dozen red roses. She did something that she had never done before. She went to her father's last resting place on his birthday and laid the roses down at his headstone. She had never visited her father's grave site before now. She read his headstone: "*Loving, devoted husband and father. Gone too soon.*" She kneeled down and put her right hand on his headstone.

"Daddy, I know you're looking down at me. I hate I never got the chance to know you. Jamila always told me you stood on loyalty. She stressed it to me. So I try to walk in both of your footsteps, dad. I never betrayed her. I did everything she asked me to do. But she feels I betrayed her, and all I ever did was love her."

"Stop lying to my father."

When Symone got up and turned around, Jamila was standing a few feet back from her with two dozen white and yellow roses. Jamila walked past Symone and laid her roses down next to Symone's roses.

"Happy Birthday, Daddy. I love you and miss you," Jamila said, kissed two of her fingers and gently touched her two fingers to his headstone. Jamila stood up and looked Symone in the face. Symone looked to the left and saw Masi and Lorenzo standing by the car.

"Jamila, I didn't lie to our father, because I did not betray you at all. I was loyal to you to the very end."

"How were you loyal to me? By going behind my back and starting your own family in Brooklyn, Symone?"

"I didn't start my family, Jamila, until you banished me from yours. The only thing I did was, have some guys sell heroin for me in Brooklyn, that's all. I was at *Jelani's* every day and night taking care of the family business. Not one time have I ever crossed you, and it wasn't right for you to have Lorenzo come to *Passion's* with Tasha, Crystal and Masi and belittle me by taking my chain at gunpoint and banish me from the family by smoking a cigar and smiling in my face. My big sister sent her goons at me to embarrass me like I wasn't shit. How do you think that made me feel after I did what he couldn't do when you went to prison? I kept the LaCross Family name alive while he was in the hospital. I've killed for this family. All I wanted to do was, make you proud. But you know what hurt the most? You never picked up the phone and called me to find out what happened, to see if it was true or not. You just threw me to the side like I wasn't shit to you."

"I should have called you. You're right, but Lorenzo's been my second-in-command from day one, so I took his word. He never gave me a reason not to trust him at all."

"Well, there's a first time for everything. Just so you know, he lied against me. I don't know why, but he did, I swear on daddy."

"That still don't justify you shooting up my restaurant and everything else you did."

"I was hurt. I was in my emotions. I was angry. I felt betrayed. I looked up to you, and you fucked me up." Symone had tears in her eyes as she talked to Jamila. For the first time, she let all of her emotions go.

"Symone, I'm sorry. I am." Jamila opened her arms and Symone gave her a hug, crying on her shoulder. Lorenzo and Masi just watched them hug from the car.

"Symone, please forgive me. I will never let anyone come between us again. I didn't know Lorenzo or Tasha treated you that way. Symone, I love you. I really do."

Symone pushed back from Jamila and looked up at her.

"You don't love me, because a few days ago you would have had me killed, and it's been too many broken walls to go back in the past and not enough concrete and steel to rebuild a future. You once told me when someone is disloyal, no matter who they are, death has a number for them and the only way to fix a broken plate is to kill the person who broke it. Find out the truth from your second-in-command and let death collect his number to show me you love me." Symone kissed Jamila's cheek and left her standing at their father's grave, not looking back.

Chapter Thirty-Five

Jamila walked into her office and locked the door behind her. She kept asking herself, "Why would Lorenzo lie against Symone? What would he have to gain by turning two sisters against each other by putting us at war? It just doesn't make sense." She never questioned Lorenzo's loyalty, but she should have talked to Symone before making a judgement call against her. She went over all of the books for her establishment for the five years that she had been in prison, while Symone was in charge of the family, and not one thing came up short. Nothing was out of place. Jamila looked pensive. After a few minutes, she picked up the phone and called Masi. He picked up after two rings.

"Hello, Masi, come to my office, we need to talk." Jamila hung up and put her gun on her desk. She walked to her bar and got a bottle of Cîroc. She sat down at her desk and took two shots. That's when Masi knocked at her office door. She got up and unlocked her door.

"Masi, come in and have a seat."

Masi noticed the gun on her desk and the bottle of Cîroc.

"Masi, we need to talk and I want to know the truth. Do you understand me?"

Masi looked into Jamila's eyes.

"Yes, I do."

"How was Symone when she was the head of my family?"

Masi closed his eyes and opened them, looking at Jamila.

"She was very ruthless. She had no understanding. There were times when I asked myself, '*Who's gonna die today?*' You know the saying: '*Hell has a place for you*'? Jamila, there's a special place for Symone picked out in hell for the river of blood and the souls she has taken. She killed children to make a point."

"Masi, did she ever try to turn any of you against me, or did she ever try to take my place?"

"Never, she always said: 'My sister's Queendom will not fall under my watch'. She made sure your money was counted to a tee, and every dime was right. When she found out that you had a price on your head, she went bananas. If she sent us to kidnap somebody, she had already made up in her mind that person was gonna die. She did what she had to do to get the information she needed to know. She had no limits. Her stories are worse than the boogyman's. I remember Joe Scott hanging upside down from a balcony twenty-six floors up while she calmly ate a green apple. She gave him a choice: sign everything over to her or see if he could fly. He signed everything over to her, then before walking out she killed his two bodyguards."

Jamila sat quietly, listening to Masi tell his stories about Symone and how she came up.

"Masi, tell me about the drugs in Brooklyn she started selling."

"Oso asked her one day if she could move some work for him and she said *yes*. She didn't want your money mixed up with Oso's, so she had some guys in Brooklyn sell it. She didn't want us to touch it because she said you did not want heroin in Queens, and she wasn't gonna disrespect you by having your men selling heroin in Brooklyn behind your back."

"The day Lorenzo took her chain, what happened that night?"

"To be honest, that shit was foul. We walked into *Passion's* that night. Everything was going good. When we reached the office, Lorenzo was already in there smoking a cigar with a white suit on, like he was the new Don.

"He told me and Muscle to leave. We left him and Symone in there talking. Tasha and Crystal came and got us and brought us through the back door to the office. Tasha told us that Symone was about to be banished from the family, and if she tries anything, Lorenzo told us to kill her. Still, to this day, I don't know what she did, but I don't ask questions. I just follow orders."

"Masi, when Lorenzo took control of the family, how was he?"

"He wasn't as strict as Symone. He just wanted to be the man. He acted like a king, fucking girls, and had us following him around like puppies. That's why Symone was able to catch him down bad. She knew all she needed was a bad bitch, because he was weak for pussy, and then the trap was laid out."

144

"I don't understand. Why would he tell me she started her own family when she didn't?"

Masi turned his head and looked down at the ground when she said that.

"Masi, when someone looks down at the ground, that means that they are either hiding something or they are thinking of a lie to tell. What are you not telling me?"

Masi took a deep breath.

"Lorenzo said one time when he was drunk that Symone was getting too big and too powerful. Honestly, I think he was just hating on her and wanted her out of the way."

"Masi, thank you for your honesty. This is *our* conversation, and no one will ever know about it. You can go now."

Masi got up, looked at Jamila and walked out the door. Jamila took another shot before going back into her thoughts.

***

Symone got a phone call earlier that day telling her that Gino Sabrano would see her. She let Halo know that she would be gone for the day to a very important meeting. She had her eyes closed as she rode in the back of the limo. It was a two-and-a-half-hour drive to his house. When the limo came to a stop and her door opened, there were two men standing outside her door.

"Ms. Rose, please follow us this way. Mr. Sabrano is waiting for you."

Symone looked at both men. "Sure, after you, gentlemen."

They walked Symone through a path through the woods to the far side of the property where Gino Sabrano stood in a river, fishing with green knee-high rubber boots on. He looked at her.

"Ms. Rose, I don't know if I have your size right but please come out here and join me."

Symone was at a loss for words and confused.

When she turned around, one of Mr. Sabrano's guards had a pair of rubber boots for her to put on. She put them on and went out into the river to talk to Mr. Sabrano.

"How are you, Symone?"

"I'm good today. So, is this something you do all the time?"

"Symone, heaven is what you make it. Symone, when you imagine heaven, you imagine a beautiful place, a peaceful place, and a quiet place. Out here where I am is beautiful, peaceful, and quiet, so I guess you can call this my little piece of heaven. Now tell me, what brings you way out here to see me?"

"I'm running low on heroin and I need a new supplier, and I was wondering if you could help me out with that."

"I believe I can help you out with that problem. But now that you are back with *the Seven*, why don't you ask the Queen Don?"

"Because I don't want to be under her wing, and I don't want her holding anything over my head. I made a name for myself five years ago when she was in prison, and I don't want my respect from the Mafia because my name is affiliated with hers. I want respect because I earned my stripes, Mr. Sabrano."

"You did earn your stripes, Symone, and nobody can deny that, but you do know nothing in the Mafia is free. Your sister, Red Invee, had to pay Mayor Oakland and Kent Washington a visit that they would never come back from, to make her who she is today. So now I tell you, I need someone to disappear. If you do this for me, I'll give you their property and the supplier you want. Now, there is a deadline if you accept this offer that I bring to you today. Before I tell you who it is, understand everyone has their motives for what they do. Symone, your name carries a lot of weight, and you are a famous female, just like your sister. Sometimes patience is the best answer to a deadly enemy."

"Mr. Sabrano, who is it that you want me to kill?"

"Glen Teliono."

Nonplussed, Symone looked at him.

"Symone, listen to what I'm about to tell you. The hardest thing in the Mafia is to learn which bridges to cross and which bridges to burn. Symone if you cross my bridge, you will forever be protected, but if you burn my bridge I will erase the thought and memory of the Rose Family, like your family never existed. It's like taking the blue pill or the red pill. The truth or a lie."

Symone looked at Mr. Sabrano.

"I'm gonna choose to cross your bridge, Mr. Sabrano."

Mr. Sabrano nodded as he threw his fishing line back into the water.

Chapter Thirty-Six

Amber walked to the front desk to receive her property.

"Now Amber, you be safe out there. I don't want to see you back in here."

"Sergeant Robinson, I promise you I will never come back to this place. Hell to the no." Amber walked out the building and looked up at the sky for the first time in five years. The sky was a perfect blue as the sunrays touched her face. Amber walked through the prison gates and saw a black stretch Hummer-limo waiting outside. She looked at the limo as the doors opened. Jamila stepped out with a smile on her face as she walked to Amber.

"Hello, beautiful, how are you? Does it feel good to be free?"

Amber just smiled as she walked up to Jamila and gave her a long hug.

"Hello, Jamila. And yes, it feels really good to be free."

"Trust me, I know the feeling. Come on, let's go. I have a dinner being prepared for you at the restaurant. I know you want some real food in your system."

"You know I do. I can't wait." Jamila put her hand on Amber's lower back as she stepped into the limo.

"Come on, let's go."

***

"Mr. Sabrano, do you think Rose will pull it off?"

"Killing Glen Teliono will be easy for her. The challenge to her will be her loyalty to him and the line I just made her cross. I need to know if she can be who I need her to be. I believe in her, and I don't need her emotions standing in the way of her greatness. I believe she can go much further than Jamila with the right guidance in time, Allen."

"There's no doubt in my mind that she won't pull it off now that you've broke it down to me like that, but I do have a question: How can you trust someone like her if she's willing to kill a loyal man just to cross your bridge?"

"It's not about crossing my bridge. It's about feeding her family and people in Brooklyn. That's why she's gonna do it. Her loyalty is to her people, and I respect that."

"How long does she have to do the job?"

"Three weeks. I'm not worried about her because I could tell by the look in her eyes her mind was made up. One thing you must know is that Symone is more ruthless than Jamila. I saw the look in her eyes when she put her gun to Jamila's head. If I wasn't there, Jamila would have been a dead moolie. Remember this, Allen: Blood makes you related, loyalty makes you family, and the wall of loyalty between them has broken down. Now come on, I would like to eat what I caught today."

"I'm right behind you, Mr. Sabrano."

Chapter Thirty-Seven

"You know, you guys really need to learn the game before I take all of your paper. I like free money." Vinnie laughed as he picked the money up off the pool table.

"Who next? One of you know how to play the game." Vinnie stopped talking when he saw Jamila walk through the pool hall door with Masi and Tasha by her side. He laid his pool stick down on the table, as he walked toward Jamila.

"Now ain't this a surprise? The Queen herself just walked through the doors. Tell me, Queen Don, what brings you by?" Vinnie said as he gave her a hug and kiss on the cheek.

"Good afternoon, gentlemen, and I came to talk to you, Mr. Lenacci. If you are not busy, I have a question that you may be able to answer."

"I'm never busy when it comes down to you. Sure, come to my back office. I always have time for you."

Once in the back office, Vinnie pulled out a chair for Jamila to sit in, and he sat down in a chair right in front of her.

"So, tell me, Ms. LaCross, what can I do for you?"

"I have a question that I feel you can answer for me."

"Ask away. I'm all ears."

"The day we planned to have Alex killed, what made you make that decision? To kill the man you'd known for years?"

"Red Invee, our war was the worst war my family has ever been through. We were so comfortable in our ways. We just knew no one would ever try us, but the day Tony got killed we wanted blood. We wanted everybody that was responsible dead. We noticed you didn't back down, especially when we were losing men on both sides, more men from my family—Sonny, Tony, and others. I just knew it was time to end this war. Alex tried to walk in shoes that were too big for his feet. It wasn't about Alex and what he wanted. It was about what was best for the Lenacci Family, and what was right. He didn't want to stop. The choice was hard but necessary. It had to be done. The question I had to ask myself was: 'One man's life or multiple men's lives over one man's decisions? When I went to talk to

Frankie and decided to set Alex up, it wasn't about our past or the bread we broke. It was about my family's future and the lives I would be saving. Sometimes the hardest decisions to make are the ones we overlook. I don't know why you came and asked me this today but let me tell you this—everyone wants to be the boss and every soldier is not loyal. Sometimes it takes certain situations to show you where somebody really stands with you, and their true colors sometimes. You will never see their true intentions until it's too late."

"Thank you, Vinnie, for cleaning that up for me. Last week I had a meeting with Gino Sabrano and Symone Rose. At this meeting I ordered the Scott Family and the Teliono Family to come back to *the Seven*, as well as the Rose Family. I made the Rose Family pay sanctions, fines, and dues. The total amount was three million, three hundred thousand dollars. I will have Tasha and Masi bring the other four families their share of the money. The money will be split down the middle between the other four families and passed out this week. Thank you for your advice, Mr. Lenacci."

"Anytime, Ms. LaCross."

Vinnie got up, shook Jamila's hand, and gave her a kiss on the cheek as he let her hand go. He watched her as she stepped out his office.

***

Symone sat in the backseat of the Range Rover and watched Detective Green cook on the grill at the park, as his wife pushed their children on the swing set.

"It would be nothing for us to walk over there and kill them right now, Ms. Rose."

"No, Pistol, I don't want them dead. I want to talk to him first and let him know what he has to lose. When he starts walking this way, I want you to step outside the Range Rover and point to Iceman and Slim at the picnic table. Then show him your gun and let him know I need to have a word with him, or we can go another route."

"I got you, Ms. Rose, I know what to do."

***

"Baby, your food smells so good. I can't wait to eat."

"It will be ready in a few minutes, beautiful. Um—while the kids are playing on the seesaw, would you mind watching the food? I left the sauce and two pans in the car, but the food won't be ready for about fifteen minutes, my love, unless you want to walk to the car and get that stuff for me."

"I'm not walking to the car in that hot ass sun."

"I got the food, bae." Officer Green kissed his wife and walked toward his car. He noticed the Range Rover and Pistol standing outside of it with his hand on his gun. He looked back at his wife and kids.

"Don't do no stupid shit, Detective Green. I can see it in your eyes. Look over at the picnic table. We have guys everywhere. Now, someone wants to talk to you. We can do this my way and take five minutes out of your time, or your way and have you praying for your family's lives. What is it gonna be, Detective Green?"

Detective Green looked at Pistol and walked past him as Pistol opened the door to the Range Rover for him to get in.

"I'm finally in your presence, Ms. Rose."

"How are you, Detective Green?"

"I'm fine, and I'm not a detective anymore."

"I'm sorry to hear that."

"So, this is what you do? Threaten my family for me to come talk to you?"

"Officer Green, your daughters are playing on the seesaw and your wife is cooking on the grill, talking to a friend. They don't seem threatened at all. They don't even know that we're having this conversation."

"Do you mind if we make this conversation short so that I can get back to my family?"

"Let me get to the point then, Officer Green. I have killed more people over the years than John Gott, Al Capone, and Sammy "The

Bull". I'm really New York's fucking nightmare. Every time you do a stakeout or try to get something against me, you are rolling dice, gambling with your life and your family's. When you crap out, I'm not only coming for your blood but your family's too. I have no understanding for bullshit, and when I get on the fuck shit, I get on it."

Officer Green couldn't believe how beautiful Symone was, and how calm she talked to him. He knew her threats were real and deadly as he listened to every word that she said. "Don't try to earn your stripes by coming after me, because it won't work. It's not gonna go well. I will always be two steps ahead of you. The first warning was your dog's head in a pot. I'm giving you this second warning right now, and I'm gonna show you how it's going to end if I have to see you face to face again." Symone pulled out her own phone and showed Officer Green the pictures of the late KT's body, and his mother, sister, and son as they hung from chains, with gunshot wounds to the chest and head.

"The dead nigga you're seeing in the pics was one of my lieutenants, but he strayed from the fold and betrayed me. That explains why you see him dead in the photos. I made sure his mother, sister, and son accompanied him in death. Now, Officer Green, hear me well, I will make you watch me kill your family one by one, then I will beat you to death last. Don't push me, please don't. I have no limits. I don't care how much you hate me, but love your family more than you hate me."

Officer Green looked at Symone, not saying a word. Symone tapped on the window two times, and Pistol opened the door for Officer Green to step out. Pistol got in the driver's seat of the Range Rover, and Officer Green watched as they drove off.

Chapter Thirty-Eight

Jamila walked up to Steve as he was washing the limos in the back of the restaurant. She took a seat in a chair by the door. He did not notice her watching him. She had the logbook in her hands, going over it. When he turned around, he noticed her sitting there.

"I'm sorry, Ms. LaCross. I didn't know you were out here. Is there somewhere you need to go? I was just out here washing the limos, that's all."

"No, I don't have anywhere to go right now. I just need to ask you some questions. As a matter of fact, yeah, go get the Mercedes and let's go for a ride. I'll be right here waiting for you."

"Yes, Ms. LaCross."

When Steve pulled up in the Mercedes, he got out and opened the back door for Jamila to get in.

"Ms. LaCross, where are we going?"

"I just want to go for a drive. We need to talk. Steve, you have been my driver for seven years now, give or take."

"Just about, Ms. LaCross."

"How would you like a new position, maybe work one of the floors for me?"

"I would like that."

"Good. I like to give rewards to my loyal workers, the ones I should never have to second guess. See, I know I can trust you, Steve. However, what I don't understand is—when you were driving for Symone while I was locked up, you wrote everything down in the logbook. I went through them, and last year when you were driving for Lorenzo, you didn't write down all of your locations. Why is that?"

"Lorenzo told me not to. He said it wasn't important, plus he said the FBI and DEA would love to get their hands on that book, so he stopped me from writing in them."

"He made a good point. Have you started writing in the logbook since you've been driving me around again?"

"Yes, Ms. LaCross, I have."

SAYNOMORE

"I don't understand why you start back when you start driving me around, but you wouldn't write in the logbook when you drove Lorenzo around, yet you also wrote in the logbook when you drove Symone around."

"I just thought that was what you wanted me to do, Ms. La-Cross."

"Do you remember the old road to Frankie's house?"

"Yes, Ms. LaCross, the private road."

"Yes, head that way for me. There's something I need to see. So, do you remember some of the places that Lorenzo had you take him to."

"The only places I took him to was *Destiny's*, *Passion's*, *Jelani's*, and his house"

"And that's all, Steve?"

"Yes, Ms. LaCross, that's it."

"So, there was no reason to write anything down. Are you sure, Steve?"

"Yes, I am, Ms. LaCross."

"I really appreciate your honesty. Do you see that white house to the left?"

"Yes."

"Pull over there for me, but drive around the back of the house."

When they drove around to the back of the house, Steve stopped the car by an oak tree.

"Turn the car off. I'll be right back."

Jamila opened the car door. She had her gun in her hand. Steve leaned over to get his cell phone out of the glove box when Jamila opened his car door.

"Steve, you fucked up!" Jamila said, as she pointed her gun at him. "You lied to me." Jamila pulled the trigger with a scowl. Four gunshots went off. Steve's body jerked in agony from the impact of the bullets as his phone fell from his hand. Jamila stepped back as Steve's body rolled out of the driver's side of the car. Steve looked up at Jamila as he tried to say something, but blood bubbles were coming out of his mouth. Jamila squatted over him.

"What was the first rule, Steve? *You fuck up the first time, you die.* I found the log-in sheet you had in your desk drawer. You forgot to throw it away. 114 Herringbone Dr.—you went there three times with Lorenzo, *why*? I don't know, but I'll figure it out."

Steve was taking short breaths when he got the got the word: *'Diablo'* out of his mouth. Jamila put the gun to his head.

"You're fucking lying!" She pulled the trigger one more time and blew his brains out. She got up, got in the car and zoomed off, leaving him there lying dead in his own blood.

***

Symone sat in her office watching the BET awards, as a new young artist named Gizmo was on stage performing his new hit— *Gangstas Passion.* She was bobbing her head to the rhythm of the beat, and she started singing along with him: "*Bet you say they love me I'm like fuck it / I don't trust it niggas tellin lies I'm televised / so I'm like fuck it 285 with them bricks hoping I get lucky.*" She stopped singing when Halo walked into her office. Symone was still vibing to Gizmo's song and to the beat, though.

"Yo, who's that rocking the stage, Rose?"

"He's new. His name is Gizmo and he got bars. You know what, Halo? There are so many talented young black men in Brooklyn. I think I'm gonna give them a shot. I think I wanna open up a record label."

"What? You? Wanna open a record label? And what would you call it?"

"Hustle Money Ent."

"Are you dead ass serious, Rose?"

"I am, and you have that old record label that went out of business on 127th and Park. I think it was called Horrorville Records."

"Yeah, I remember. I know exactly where that place is."

"Go check it out, Halo, and if it's for sale, buy the building. Get everything prepared inside and out. Get everything you need. I want top-of-the-line equipment, and I want a big ass sign that says: *Hustle Money Ent 440.*"

"OK. I'm gonna go get on that now while it's still early. I'll let you know what's up when I come back."

"I'll be waiting for you."

***

Glen Teliono was looking out his window at the docks.

"Look at all of this, Danny, I own it all. Everything you see out there I get a piece of."

"You're right. That's what I don't understand. I mean why did you need Rose? I've been racking my brain trying to figure it out."

"Because you don't see the big picture. The niggas in the Brooklyn projects love her, so we use her to get to them and it's a win-win for us. I don't give a fuck about being partners with Rose. I don't give a fuck about it. I'm just using her 'cause I see the bigger picture. I see money when I talk to her. When you see that, Danny, you'll see what I see, and you won't be racking your damn brain. Just like my father saw these docks thirty years ago, they weren't shit back then. Now look at them. Everyone comes to see me because my docks happen to be the only way for them to come get their dope, and I get a piece of everything. It's about what you can gain, Danny. Why do you think Gino Sabrano is in those hills? It's simply because he saw the five boroughs for what they were. He saw those niggers for what they were—with their explosive athletic skills, their colorful clothes, loud music playing and their rhythm, and—the best part—drug using assets. So, he put the five families together, and we all got a piece of the pie."

"You make a good point, Glen, but now you got a nigger as the Queen Don and her little sister running shit too. The Italians are taking all this from niggers."

"Is that what you think, Danny? Jamila don't run shit. She's just a face, nothing else, and that's just to get some heat off our backs. When word got back to Gino Sabrano about her, he saw the bigger picture and he green-lighted her to be a part of the families. It was never about no fucking vote. He had the last say-so in the matter. A nigger running the mob? I don't care what it looks like. Open your eyes, Danny." Glen got up, opened his office window and looked out over the docks.

SAYNOMORE

Chapter Thirty-Nine

Muscle knocked on the door to Jamila's office before opening the door.

"Ms. LaCross, you wanted to see me?"

"Yes, I did. Come in and have a seat, Muscle." Muscle could tell by her vibe what type of meeting this was.

"Muscle, tell me, how long have you been a part of this family?"

"From day one."

"Have I ever been unfair to you, Muscle?"

"No, you have always been fair to me."

"I would never ask you to do nothing I wouldn't do myself, but today I'm going to ask you to do something for me and this will be between me and you. I don't want nobody else to know about this. This is for your ears alone, Muscle." Jamila looked at Muscle when she said this, and he looked back at her. Muscle nodded at her.

"I want you to go to the farm, to the far end and dig me an eight-foot deep hole and wait for me. And when I come back there, the person I'm with is the one who is going in the hole."

"When do you want me to dig the hole?"

"You can leave today and start, and remember—don't tell nobody what I just told you. I need this done tonight, no later than nine p.m., maybe ten p.m."

"I won't tell nobody, Ms. LaCross."

"I trust that you won't, Muscle." Muscle got up and walked out of Jamila's office. He headed to the farm like she asked him to. As Muscle was walking out, Lorenzo was walking into Jamila's office.

"Hey, what's up, Jamila? I see you been busy the last couple of days," Lorenzo said as he walked to the bar to get himself something to drink.

"Yes, I've had a very busy and interesting week."

"What was Muscle doing up here?"

"I have him digging his own grave. I found out that he's been disloyal, and it's sad 'cause he's been by my side from day one."

"What do you mean *disloyal*?"

"It's not important, Lorenzo. As a matter of fact, you can come with me when I go and confront him, so you will know exactly why I'm gonna kill him and you will know why I did what I did. But what I need for you to do for me, Lorenzo, is go to the waste plant and count all the kilos and make sure our money count is right. I want to get another shipment, and I need to know how much to order."

"OK. I'm gonna go take care of that now."

"Lorenzo, try to be back by seven-thirty p.m., so that we can go take care of that business at the farm."

"I'll be back by then, Jamila."

Jamila watched as Lorenzo got up and walked out of her office.

***

Symone was in a deep thought when Slim Boogie walked into her office.

"Symone, this place is fly. I still can't get out of my head how you turned up. Big facts. You did the one-hundred-yard dash."

"No, Slim, we did the hundred-yard dash together. I just held it down while you was in the hospital."

"Symone, you are the real one, but I can tell you have got a lot on your mind."

"Yeah, someone dropped a heavy load on me, Slim."

"What did they say to you, Symone?"

"They told me in the Mafia I need to learn which bridges to cross and which bridges to burn, then he gave me a choice, so I decided to cross his bridge and burn the one I was on. One thing I've learned, Slim, is: you can't have no feelings in the mob. Trust, love, and emotions can get you killed."

"So how are you gonna burn a bridge, Symone."

"Slim, there is only one way to burn a bridge in the mob." Symone stood up from her desk and lit her Black and Mild.

"When you burn a bridge in the mob, you make sure everything turns into ashes. Go tell Iceman and Pistol it's time to turn a bridge into ashes."

162

***

Missing You—by Whitney Houston—was playing in the background while Jamila took shots of Patron as she looked at the picture of her and Lorenzo that they took together a few years back. She was reminiscing about all the good times they'd had; from the time they were dancing in the club up until the time they were play fighting. She also cast her mind back to one occasion when he took a bite of her sandwich. She recalled the classes they took together in college, and how Lorenzo had been her emotional support. She had tears in her eyes, as she thought about everything that they had been through. She looked at her office floor at the spot where Lorenzo got shot and she was holding his hand, begging him to fight it, telling him she was going to get help. She wiped the tears from her eyes, picked up her black 9mm and put it in her bag as she left her office, leaving Whitney Houston's song playing on repeat. She didn't talk to anybody, as she walked the main floor of the restaurant right out front to the car where Lorenzo was waiting for her.

"Jamila, is something bothering you?"

"Yes, but I don't want to talk about it. Is everything good with the cocaine?"

"Yes, everything is good and the money counted as well."

"How many kilos do we have?"

"Two-fifty."

"Good. Now, let's go to the farm."

"So what did Muscle do?"

"He was disloyal, and I caught him in multiple lies. It's sad because his actions show that he was in it only for himself, and he got members of our family killed behind his actions." Jamila didn't say anything else on the rest of the ride to the farm.

***

It was a chill breeze as the wind blew over the water. Symone stood at the far end of the docks, looking at the reflection of the moonlight upon the midnight water as she was waiting for Glen Teliono to meet her there. She pulled out a Black and Mild, and lit it as she looked at the two men walking her way under the dock lights. The only thing that kept replaying in her mind was, learning which bridges to cross and which bridges to burn. Glen Teliono walked up to Symone, hugged her and gave her a kiss on each cheek.

"Symone, I came when you told me it was important, that you needed to see me tonight. What's going on?"

Symone looked at Danny, not saying a word.

"Don't worry about Danny. He's my second-in-command. You can trust him. He is a made man."

"Mr. Teliono, anybody you bring to my table I trust. I trust your judgement. I called you out here because earlier this week I had a conversation with Gino Sabrano and your name came up. I wasn't going to tell you about this conversation, but I couldn't keep it to myself knowing you are my ally."

Glen Teliono looked at Danny, then back at Symone.

"One thing Mr. Sabrano kept stressing was *which bridge to cross and which bridge to burn.*"

"Why did he have you come talk to him about me?"

"I guess because I'm backing you up, so why did he bring your name up to me?"

***

Jamila opened the door to step out of the car at the farm.

"So where is Muscle, Jamila? I see his car but I don't see him anywhere around."

"He's at the far end of the farm. I had him dig the hole over there. Come on, let's go meet him back there, Lorenzo."

Jamila and Lorenzo walked to the far end of the farm quietly until they reached the woods.

"Do you remember the first time we walked through these woods, Lorenzo?"

"Yeah, you said someday we will be burying someone in these woods."

Jamila didn't show it but she had tears running down her face when he said that.

"Come on, Lorenzo, Muscle is standing over there."

Jamila and Lorenzo walked over to Muscle as he was holding the shovel in his hand. Lorenzo looked at how deep the hole was, and looked back at Jamila, and came to realize it was for him. He sighed before he spoke.

"I've been thinking about this for a long time now, a twenty-eight-year-old friendship that I fucked up. Over what? Once the foundation of trust is broken, there is no rebuilding it. No matter how I try to seal the patches up, I know what you stand on, Jamila, and I know why trust and loyalty is so valuable to you. Because your father was killed behind disloyalty."

"I love you, Lorenzo, and I took your word over my blood sister's. You could never do no wrong in my eyes. Why, Lorenzo? Why did you put me in this position? You was my fucking brother. Do you know the hole you ripped in my soul and how much it hurt me when I went to 114 Herringbone Dr. and I found out all along that Felipe and Jatavious Stone killed my father and you knew about it for years! Now I know why you told Frankie I need to stop digging up my past, because you didn't want this to come to the light. Not only that, but now I know why you let Symone run the family. It wasn't because I told you to go MIA. It was because you didn't want to have to choose between us. But you did choose sides, Lorenzo, when he had me stabbed up in prison and put a price on my head. You still talked to him day after day. You chose sides then. You picked him over me." Jamila had tears in her eyes as she talked to Lorenzo, letting her emotions out. She pulled her gun out, holding it tight as she looked at Lorenzo.

"You're right. I knew they killed your father. I remember hearing my father talk about it. How could I tell you that my father did business with the men that killed your father?"

"Lorenzo, this is deeper than my father's death and your father's business. This is about you and me. It has more to do with the choice you made to continue doing business with that man and his family."

Lorenzo pulled his gun out and looked at Jamila. Muscle just watched them both. He knew he had no place in the conversation.

"Lorenzo, what was the purpose of turning Symone, my sister, against me and me against her?"

Lorenzo just looked at Jamila and lowered his head.

***

"I don't know why he brought it up. What else did he say to you?"

"It's really not important, Mr. Teliono. What's important is that I burnt an old bridge and crossed a new one."

Glen looked at Danny and back at Symone.

"What do you mean by that?"

"This," Symone said, and pulled out her Glock 9mm, pointing it at Glen and Danny.

"You are on my docks. Do you think you can kill me and get away with it?"

"I already have. Your two guards at the gate are dead. Iceman took care of that, and Pistol took care of your men in the office. It's just us three out here right now."

"I opened my family up to you. I backed you up, Symone!"

"No, you used me for Brooklyn and now our conversation is over, and I kill you now."

"You bitch!" Glen Teliono ran towards Symone.

Symone shot him three times in the chest, dropping him. Before Danny could do anything, his body was falling right next to Glen Teliono. Symone stood over them both and shot them in the sides of their heads. Both bodies went limp. Iceman and Pistol walked up to Symone a few minutes later without looking back.

"Get rid of their bodies. Give them watery graves with chains and bricks. All of them." After giving those instructions, Symone walked off, not looking back at Iceman or Pistol.

***

"Jamila, I'm not gonna have this conversation with you." Lorenzo looked at his gun, smiled and threw his gun in the hole.

"I would never hurt you, Jamila. I'm sorry. Muscle, don't let her kill me, do it for her. Jamila, I'm not gonna let you hold the weight of my death on your shoulders. You're not going to carry that burden around. Let's get this over with."

"Lorenzo, wait." Jamila dropped her gun on the ground and walked up to Lorenzo. She gave him a hug.

"I'm sorry, Jamila. I'm so sorry." Lorenzo kissed her on the forehead.

Jamila had her arms wrapped around Lorenzo as her head rested on his chest. She knew what had to be done, even if her heart was against it.

"I love you, Lorenzo."

"I love you more, Jamila. I'll be at the Pearly White Gates waiting for you. Stop crying, beautiful, wipe the tears from your eyes."

Jamila kissed Lorenzo on the chin and nodded. She took two steps back and looked at Muscle. Muscle pointed his gun at Lorenzo.

"Muscle, go ahead and do it," Lorenzo said. Muscle looked at Jamila for confirmation.

Jamila nodded. Three shots were let off, and Jamila watched as Lorenzo's body fell into the open grave. She let out a scream, covering her face as she looked at his dead body.

SAYNOMORE

Chapter Forty

One Week Later—

"Ms. LaCross, you wanted to see me?"

Jamila looked at Tasha as she walked into her office.

"Yes, come in and have a seat, Tasha. I know things feel strange around here without Lorenzo being around. I know how close you two were starting to become." Jamila got up, walked around her desk and sat next to Tasha.

"Tasha, no one was closer to Lorenzo than me. It really hurt me to do what I had to do." Jamila took Tasha's hand in hers and looked into her eyes.

"Tasha, this goes for everyone, no matter who it is. The first sign of disloyalty—kill them, because you will be the one they're plotting to kill. Lorenzo was disloyal to me for many years, and it took for me to go to prison, for the right puzzle pieces to fall in place."

"So why is Symone still alive even though she crossed all of us and was disloyal to the family?"

"Tasha, can you tell me how Symone was disloyal to our family?"

"Look at all she did."

"But what was her very first act of disloyalty?"

"I don't know. Lorenzo never told me."

"There wasn't one, Tasha. Lorenzo started a war over jealousy and envy, and it came to the light after I did a three-week investigation, and I asked him with a witness, and he knew he was wrong, so he accepted his fate. But today, right now I bring you a blessing and a curse. I want to know now; do you want to step up and be my number two? Do you think that you can do that? Do you think that you have what it takes to run my empire when I'm not around? To think about the choices you have to make before you execute them! I trust your judgement, Tasha, but the question is: do you trust your own judgement?"

"I trust my judgement, and I know I can run your empire when you are not around. This means a lot to me, you wanting me to be your number two."

"Tasha, please don't let me down or put me in a position I don't want to be in."

"I promise you I won't, Jamila. If they kill you, they kill me."

Jamila gave Tasha a hug and a kiss on the cheek. She pulled out a two carat VVS diamond ring and put it on Tasha's finger.

"Tasha, hear me very well. Move like a boss bitch. Act like a boss bitch. Talk like a boss bitch. Always have confidence in your decisions and yourself. Once you make the call, it's finalized. Never regret your decisions, and remember—no one is bigger than the mob. Now come on, let me be the first to take a shot with my new second-in-command."

***

Gino Sabrano stepped out of his limo in front of Panache Fine Jewelry Store.

"It looks like a nice place. Let's step inside, Glenn."

Halo saw both men enter the jewelry store, and knew exactly who they were. Halo met them in the middle of the floor.

"Welcome to Panache Fine Jewelry. How may I help you?"

"You have a beautiful establishment here. My name is Gino Sabrano and I was hoping I could speak with Symone Rose."

"Hold on, Mr. Sabrano. I'll go get her for you. She's right in her office in the back. One second, please."

When Symone came walking to the main floor, she saw Mr. Sabrano and his acquaintance looking over a couple of diamond encrusted watches.

"Hello, Mr. Sabrano. How are you doing today?"

"I'm doing good, Ms. Rose. You have a beautiful establishment here." Mr. Sabrano walked up to Symone. He hugged her and gave her a kiss on each cheek.

"Thank you. I put a lot of work into this place. Let me introduce you to Halo. He's my number two."

"Halo, it's nice to meet you."

"Likewise, Mr. Sabrano."

"Symone let me introduce you to a very good friend of mine. This is Glenn Pauliani."

"Nice to meet you, Mr. Pauliani."

"No, the pleasure is all mine, Ms. Rose. I've heard a lot about you."

Symone gave him a slight smile.

"Please, follow me to my office so we can talk."

"Sure, lead the way Ms. Rose."

Mr. Sabrano took a seat in front of Symone's desk, as Mr. Pauliani sat in the seat next to him.

"Symone, I see that you have honored your word and crossed the right bridge. I never doubted you, because I know what you stand on." Symone listened to Mr. Sabrano as he talked.

"Symone, for honoring your word, I've opened another door for you. That's why I brought my friend Glenn here to meet you today."

Symone cut her eyes at Glenn just to acknowledge him.

"I wanted him to meet the diamond in the rough."

"Yes, Mr. Sabrano, I did honor my word."

"Since you've honored your word then, now I'll honor my word and give you this."

Symone looked at the yellow envelope that Mr. Sabrano was passing to her. She reached for it, opened it up, and saw the deeds to the docks.

"So, the docks are mine now?"

"As I promised you, yes, they are. I knew you would get the job done. Now you are a made woman, with my stamp."

"But what about the contact I asked you for, Mr. Sabrano?"

"He's sitting right next to you, as I promised. Everything that I promised you and agreed upon has been taken care of. Mr. Pauliani will be up here to discuss all business and agreements that you'll have. Now Symone, I have to be going. If you need anything, please reach out to me."

"Thank you for honoring your word to me, Mr. Sabrano. Thank you for taking time to come and see me, Mr. Pauliani. Mr. Sabrano,

I will be in touch." Symone walked around her desk and shook hands with Mr. Sabrano. She shook hands with Mr. Pauliani too before walking them out of her office. Halo and Symone watched as their limo pulled off.

"So, that's him, Rose?"

"Yes, Halo, that is Mr. Sabrano, and he just made me a made woman. The man that was with him is the connect that we need, and *this* right here." Symone passed Halo the manilla envelope with the deeds to the docks. That's when her phone went off with a number she didn't recognize.

"Hello."

"Hey, we need to talk face to face. Meet me under the bridge tonight at nine p.m. by yourself. The bridge is off Avon."

"OK. I'll be there." Symone hung up.

"Halo, put the deeds in the safe. I have something I need to take care of."

"Do you need me to come with you?"

"No, this I have to do alone. I'll see you tomorrow." Symone said and walked out the door.

Chapter Forty-One

Symone pulled her black BMW under the bridge and opened the door to step out. She looked around at the people sleeping next to the abandoned buildings, and the ones that stood around the trash cans as fires burned in them. It was dark outside. She sat on the hood of her car and looked at her watch. It was 8:55 p.m. She pulled out a Black and Mild, and lit it. That's when she saw the blue lights of the Mercedes Benz pull up. Jamila stepped out of her car and walked over to Symone.

"Why did you want to meet me at this location?"

"Because it's neutral grounds between me and you, and we don't have to worry about any police officers coming out of their jurisdiction to follow us, but I called you here tonight to let you know it's done. He's been dead for over a week now."

"Jamila, I know these last few years have put a hole in our relationship that might be too deep to fill, but I want to start filling it up. No matter what, you are still my older sister, and I love you, and that will never change. So I bring this to the table. I killed Glen Teliono last week, and the docks are mine now. "

"Why did you kill him? For his turf?"

"No. To cross one bridge, I had to burn another. But, I have the deeds to the docks and I'm offering you fifty percent of the property. On daddy's blood, with this agreement, that neither of us will sell our half of the property."

"Why are you doing this, Symone?"

"Jamila, I always looked up to you. I wanted to be just like you, and one man tore us apart with lies and jealousy. I just want to fix what's broken. You have a restaurant, a dog track, an ocean front property, a hotel and clubs, and a waste plant. I have a casino, strip club, and jewelry stores. You did what you said and killed the man who turned us against each other. Now, I'm trying to make things right with us. I want it to be two hearts and one beat, two bodies and one soul."

"Symone, daddy left me the dog track, but I will sign half that property over to you so that you can have a piece of our father as well."

Symone dropped her Black and Mild, and stepped on it, then walked up to Jamila and gave her a hug.

"Symone, I love you, and we gonna make this right again."

"I love you more, and I know we will." With those words they both went to their cars and drove away.

Chapter Forty-Two

Officer Green sat in the lobby with two folders in his hands, as he kept looking at the watch on his wrist to see what time it was. He had a 10:45 a.m. appointment with Senior Director Smith of the F.B.I.

"Mr. Green, Senior Director Smith will see you now."

"Alright, thank you."

"You're welcome. It's the fourth door to the right down the hall-way."

Officer Green took a deep breath before knocking on the door.

"Come in," said a voice from the other side of the door. Officer Green opened the door.

"Good morning, Senior Director Smith."

"Detective Green, nice to see you again. Come in, come in and have a seat."

"Good morning to you as well."

"Now tell me what can I do for you?"

"I would like for you to take a look at these pictures."

"Let me see what you've got there, son."

Senior Director Smith looked up at Officer Green as he was looking over the pictures.

"Green, do you know what you have here?"

"Yes, the twenty-third precinct indictment numbers for all of those crooked sons-of-bitches. I have everything I.A. would love to get their hands on."

"Does the Chief know about this?"

"No, he's with them, and if you keep reading you will see pictures of him with them. I left my jacket in his office the last time I was in there. Something wasn't right, so I recorded our conversation without his knowledge. The phone rang, and he told me he had to take the call. I left my jacket in there so I could catch his conversation on my tape recorder. Listen to the recorder. You can only hear him, but you will get the picture."

"*Yeah, hold on, Hall, Green just left out of here. Let me lock my door.*" One could hear the phone being put down on the office desk and the Chief Tadem walking to his office door, then one could hear him sitting back down at his desk.

"Yeah, I'm back, Hall. Now listen to me, you got Green still snooping around trying to get back on this case. I think we need Rose to pay him a visit face to face. I know for a fact that he takes his family to the park every weekend and cooks on the grill. She needs to be there and have a face-to-face with him before he brings all of us down. Yeah, yeah, that's what I want you to do. That sounds good to me, Hall. Let's get rid of the problem."

Officer Green cut the recorder off.

"Now sir, I have this lady and her goons pull up on me at the park with my family, and I couldn't do anything. I was trying to figure out how she knew where I was. I forgot about the tape recorder until we got home from the park and threw my jacket on the chair. That's when the tape recorder fell out. I was so busy trying to get these pictures developed that I forgot about my jacket in the trunk of the car over the weekend."

"He could have had your family killed. What the fuck was he thinking? Officer Green, it takes a brave cop to do what you are doing right now. Can I keep these to make some copies of them?"

"Yes, sir, whatever you need to do."

"Now, you know, Officer Green, I'm gonna need you to take the stand if this goes all the way."

"I'm willing to do whatever I need to do to bring all of these motherfuckers down, to let them know there's nobody bigger than the justice system."

"That's all I needed to hear, Green. Let's get these sons of bitches. Internal Affairs needed a case, and you just gave it to them. We got them on bribery, extortion, conspiracy. We got them in a knot that they cannot get loose."

Senior Director Smith got up, shook Officer Green's hand and walked him out the door. Senior Director Smith walked to his desk, picked up the phone and called the twenty-third precinct.

"Patch me through to Chief Tadem. Tell him its Senior Director Smith."

"Chief Tadem speaking."

"You need to take a ride on a ferry today to the Statue of Liberty at one p.m."

"I'll be there, sir."

Senior Director Smith hung up and leaned back in his chair as he looked over the pictures that Officer Green had brought to him.

***

Senior Director Smith was standing at the front of the ferry, looking at the waves as the ferry glided across the water when Chief Tadem walked up behind him.

"Smith."

"Tadem. You have a problem that's about to become our problem. Look at what one of yours brought to my attention today. You should be lucky I accepted his appointment. I mean if this would have gotten in Internal Affairs' hands or the wrong hands, all of your asses would be going down, and I wasn't gonna be on that ship with you." Senior Director Smith handed Chief Tadem the files.

"I also have a recording with your voice on it talking to Detective Hall. The shit you were talking about is called conspiracy, which warrants life—if not the death—sentence. Bottom line, you need to take care of this problem as soon as possible, and Tadem, I mean *take care of it*. You do it personally. I better not hear anything else about this, or next time I will send my clean-up crew, and I will clean up everything, Tadem, before I go down for a loose—fucking—string. Take care of the problem and let me know when it's done. Enjoy the rest of the ferry ride and you should try the hot dogs; they're outstanding." Senior Director Smith patted Chief Tadem on the back before walking away.

SAYNOMORE

Chapter Forty-Three

Officer Green walked into his cubicle and saw a note on his desk telling him to come and see Chief Tadem once he gets in. He put his coat on the back of his chair and went to see Chief Tadem. After two knocks, he heard Chief Tadem tell him to come in.

"Have a seat, Green, I want you to take the rookie and go by 126 and Gold, to those abandoned buildings and do a routine check this morning."

"OK. Is that all, sir?"

"Yeah, that's all. You can go now." Chief Tadem watched as he walked out of his office. Once Green was on the other side of the door, Chief Tadem picked up the phone and made a call.

***

"Hey, rookie, come on, we have a beat we need to do a perimeter check on. What's your name, kid?"

"Roger."

"Well, come on, Roger, the car is right over here. So, tell me, what made you want to join the force?"

"You know, get some bad guys off of the streets and do some good in the city. What made you join the force?"

"The same thing, but I came to realize the bad guys are not just in the streets but they're in uniform too. You never know who is who. Come on, let's do our perimeter check around the building. Let me just call it in, hold on. Dispatch, this is car 210. We are at 126 and South Ave., about to start our perimeter check."

"10-4, everything is a go."

"Come on, Roger, let's get this done."

As they walked around the side of the building, Green saw an open door to one of the abandoned buildings.

"Come on, let's take a look inside and see what's going on. Roger, keep your eyes open."

Roger looked at Green as he walked into the building. He pulled his gun out, looking back out the door to see if anybody else was around. As Green was walking, Roger pointed his gun to the back of his head and pulled the trigger. Echoes of the gunshots erupted through the warehouse as Roger fired at Green, emptying the clip into his body. Roger watched as Green's body fell to the ground. Roger pulled out his phone and called Chief Tadem.

"Yeah."

"It's done." Roger hung up his phone and pulled out his radio.

"Dispatch, this is Officer Roger requesting back-up at 126 South Ave. Officer down, suspects—two black males and one white male. Requesting back-up." Roger looked at Green's dead body and walked back to the squad car.

***

Roger sat in Chief Tadem's office with Internal Affairs.

"Now Roger, tell us what happened out there today. How did an officer of the law get killed?"

"We were doing a regular routine check when Green saw some guys and noticed that one of them had a gun, then he pulled his gun out and told them to '*Freeze and drop the weapon*'. Then shots were fired, but we didn't know that there was one of them behind us. That's how Green got shot. It all happened so fast."

"OK. You are going to take the next few days off, Roger, and get a psych evaluation. When we get the results back, I'll call you and let you know when to return to the force. That will be all, Officer Roger. Today wasn't your fault, so don't beat yourself up about it."

Roger nodded and walked off.

Chapter Forty-Four

Jamila looked around at the heads of all of the families. She stood up and called all of their names out.

"Symone Rose and Halo of the Rose Family, Vinnie Lenacci and Don Cap of the Lenacci Family, Joe Scott and Blue of the Scott Family, Chris Gambino and Jack of the Gambino Family, Silvio Teliono and Richard of the Teliono Family, Tony Landon and Nicky of the Landon Family. I called you all here to get a clear understanding that no one is bigger than the mob. This committee will vote on everything, and the favorite odds will win the judgement. There are seven families at this table. There will be no more wars, period! No more bloodshed from any family. We need to take back control of our streets. This last war was started over a lie from inside of my family by somebody we all know—Lorenzo. And as you can see, he's not standing next to me now, but Tasha LaCross is. Lorenzo is dead behind his disloyalty and lies. There was no punishment that he could have walked away from, after all the blood that was spilled. His only punishment was death, and I made sure it was executed. For you all at this table who don't know, Lorenzo was with me from day one. Vinnie Lenacci is a witness to this. I will not tolerate disloyalty from nobody. I will stand over your body and watch you take your last breath. I will watch you as you beg for your life. As you can see, Glen Teliono is not here tonight. It's no secret that he is dead. I don't know the ins and outs of his death, but someone here tonight does."

When Jamila said that, Gino Sabrano came walking through the door. All eyes were on him.

"Gino Sabrano, what the hell brings you from your house on the hill?" Vinnie Lenacci said, as he stood up and shook his head in astonishment.

"You know, you never really retire from the mob. You only oversee things from afar. And for the question everyone at the table wants to know, I am responsible for having Glen Teliono and his men killed. He was stealing from everyone's shipments, plus he was taxing the families."

"With the utmost respect, how do you know this, Mr. Sabrano? How do we know these allegations are true?" asked Silvio Teliono.

"Because I put peanut butter on a trap and a weasel was caught, and this is why I had Symone Rose do the job. Because I can say one thing about the LaCross Family and Rose Family—they stand on loyalty. Ms. Rose, if you will." Symone told Halo something. He got up and walked out of the room. Everyone looked at him through the CCTV camera as he opened the warehouse dock doors, and a few seconds later he pulled in a van. He got out, opened the van doors and started pulling out kilos of cocaine.

"Now Mr. Silvio," Gino Sabrano continued, "what were you saying? Or did you know about Glen Teliono's actions and kept them swept under the rug?" Silvio did not reply.

"Now, as I was saying, I have over thirty kilos from each of your shipments which is almost two-hundred kilos of dope that Glen Teliono was stealing and taxing you to use his docks. Now, the new owner of the docks is Symone Rose. Oh yeah, before you leave, take your kilos with you. Ms. LaCross, the table is yours."

"Thank you, Mr. Sabrano. I have an agreement here saying that there will be no wars amongst us, and that Mr. Sabrano will be the mediator if we need him to be. As I pass this agreement down, read it over and put your blood on the paper next to your signature. If you back out of this agreement, you will die, no questions asked. In addition, if you leave *the Seven*, your turf will be split up between the remaining families, and your family name will die with you." Jamila watched as they read and signed the agreement one by one.

"Remember, this blood makes us related but loyalty amongst us makes us family. Mr. Sabrano will keep this agreement with our blood and signatures on it. There's nothing else to say. This meeting is over."

Chapter Forty-Five

Chief Tadem was smoking his cigar, sitting on the hood of his car, waiting on Officer Roger to show up. He saw a man walking strangely in the shadows.

"Roger, is that you?"

"Yeah, it's me. I did what you said and took a detour road to make sure I wasn't followed."

"How do you feel?"

"Strange. I never killed a cop before. If this gets out, we're looking at the death sentence. This ain't gonna blow over the way we think. I don't know what I was thinking when I told you I would do it. This shit is crazy. That was a cop with a family—a wife and kids."

Chief Tadem watched Roger as he put his hands on his head in a panic mode.

"I know Internal Affairs is not gonna let this go, shit!"

"Roger, just relax, I got this. Trust me, no one's never gonna know about this. Now tell me, where's the gun at?"

"It's right here, I brought it with me like you told me to."

"OK. Good, let me have it."

Roger gave Chief Tadem the gun.

"Don't worry. Nothing's gonna come back to you, son, I promise you that." Chief Tadem put the gun into a paper bag.

"Now come here. Trust me, I got us." Chief Tadem patted Roger on the back.

"You did what we needed you to do for us today. You did a good job."

When Roger was about to wipe his face, Chief Tadem put the gun to his head and shot him two times. He watched as Roger's body fell, then he shot him two more times.

"I was gonna keep you on the team and give you a career, son. I just need eight good months and you were going to be a top-notch, Grade A detective. One job, one kill—and you fucked it up with this panicking shit. Great job. See you on the other side." Chief

Tadem looked at him one more time before getting in his car and driving off, leaving him dead with his eyes open.

***

Muscle was sitting on the steps, smoking a blunt, when Masi walked up.

"Yo, what's good, Muscle?"

"Shit, just thinking, Masi, how shit can go sideways in the blink of an eye."

"You must still be thinking how that shit went down with Lorenzo."

"Masi, I saw Lorenzo in the field. I know he'd bust his guns. He was A-1 with the gunplay. When he pulled his gun out, I knew shit was about to go crazy. I thought he was gonna go out with a bang, but just to see him throw his gun in the hole fucked me up. What blew me the most about the whole situation was to see her kiss him and hug him, and to see him kiss her forehead knowing he was about to die and just accepting that shit."

"Muscle, he knew he fucked up. There was no getting out of it. One way or another, he knew he was gonna die. That act of disloyalty cost him his life. What you have to remember is that her father was killed over disloyalty, Muscle."

"What was so foul was that he knew who killed her father and never told her. It all came out that night. That shit was sad, Masi, I didn't want to pull the trigger, but when she nodded, I gave him all headshots. Just looking at his dead body sent chills up my spine, knowing I was the one who took his life. That was my dawg, bruh."

"Muscle, you gotta let that shit go. He fumbled the ball. He fucked up. Let me hit that blunt, bruh."

Muscle pulled the blunt two more times and passed it to Masi.

"I know you heard that Jamila made Tasha her number two, Muscle."

"Yeah, I heard that, facts. That's a good look for her. That's above my pay grade. I don't ask no questions. I just shoot when I'm told to."

"I hear you, Muscle. I guess they're on their girl power shit. Look, I pulled up because Jamila want us to come by *Jelani's*."

"Word, what she got going on?"

"I don't even know. Tasha hit my line and told me to be there at two. She told me to bring you."

"Fuck it. Come on, let's see what they got going on, Masi."

***

Senior Director Smith was looking at his phone as Chief Tadem called him. He picked up and answered with a deep voice.

"Senior Director Smith, is this a secure line that we can talk on?"

"Let me call you right back on another line." Within thirty seconds Chief Tadem was on a secure line with Senior Director Smith.

"Tell me that our little problem has been eradicated?"

"Yeah, was calling to let you know that the loose string has been tied."

"Chief Tadem, let me be very clear as to what I'm about to tell you, the next time my livelihood is jeopardized over your sloppiness, the next spark you see is going to be a fatal one. There are rules to this life, and the smallest slip-up will get a needle in your arm. Tighten up. I don't want to have this conversation again."

"I understand, sir."

Senior Director Smith hung up the phone, picked up a file that was on his desk and started reading over it.

SAYNOMORE

Chapter Forty-Six

It was 1 p.m. when Detective Hall walked into Detective Green's office holding a box. There was a grim expression on his face. He put the box on Green's desk as he picked up a picture of Green with his wife and children, and looked at how happy they all were.

"Damn, Green, I told you to leave this case alone. I knew how this was gonna end." He put the picture in the box along with the rest of Green's belongings. He stopped to read over a file that Green had locked away in his filing cabinet.

'Cindy Morris—witness to Det. Boatman's murder'. Inside the file was a small tape of their conversation. Hall reached into the box, pulled out the tape recorder that Green had in his property, and put the tape into the recorder so that he could hear the conversation. Detective Hall sat down at Green's desk and pressed *play* on the recorder.

Det. Green: July 8th 2:51p.m. This is Detective Green interviewing Ms. Cindy Morris, who witnessed the murder of Detective Deontay Boatman. Ms. Morris, you reached out to me, telling me that you had information about Detective Boatman's murder. Explain to me what you saw on that fatal night.

Cindy took a deep breath before speaking.

Cindy Morris: I'm a bartender at Rayon's Bar. My shift was just ending and I gave Rayon what I took in from the bar and started walking up the street. I wanted to light a cigarette, but it was too windy, so I stepped into the doorway of an apartment building. That's when I saw a female walking up the block with a gun in her hand—

Det. Green: Alright, stop for a second. Ms. Morris, can you describe this female for me?

Cindy Morris: She was built like—I mean she couldn't have weighed no more than 138-140 pounds at the most. She was probably five foot six or five foot seven inches tall. She was light-skinned.

Det. Green: Do you know what color her hair was?

Cindy Morris: I can't remember, but I know it was long. It was either in kinky twists or braids.

Det. Green: Alright, continue, tell me what you saw.

Cindy Morris: When she walked up to the car, the detective was busy doing something because he didn't notice her.

Det. Green: Ms. Morris, can you tell me which hand the gun was in?

Cindy Morris: It was in her right hand.

Det. Green: OK. Thank you. You can continue telling me what you saw.

Cindy Morris: Where I was standing, I was directly across the street from where it happened. She said something to him.

Det. Green: Do you know what she said to him?

Cindy Morris: I couldn't make out exactly what she said to him, but I do remember hearing a name.

Det. Green: What was the name that you heard?

Cindy Morris: She mumbled something then I remember hearing the name *Lorenzo.* That's when she started shooting. She poured something in the car and set it on fire and then she took off running. I remember her getting into a car. The car stopped in front of an elderly lady and she shot her two times and then the car sped off.

Det. Green: Ms. Morris, if I was to show you some pictures do you think you would be able to recognize the shooter?

Cindy Morris: I'll try.

(*Det. Green pulls out three pictures that are in a folder and places them on the desk in front of Ms. Morris.*)

Det Green: Do you recognize any of these females as the shooter?

(*Ms. Morris points to Symone.*)

Det. Green: Ms. Morris, do you know who this is you just pointed at?

Cindy Morris: No, I do not.

Det. Green: You might not know the face, but you know the name. This is Symone LaCross of the LaCross Family, and the name that you heard her say is the gentleman right here, Lorenzo LaCross, and this picture is her sister, Jamila LaCross, the head of the family.

You are the lone witness to the assassination of Detective Boatman. Now, I have to ask you something very important. The night that you witnessed this assassination, were you on any narcotics or were you under the influence of any kind of alcohol?

(*Ms. Morris pauses for a second before she answers that question.*)

Det. Green: Ms. Morris, I want you to be honest with me. This is very important.

Cindy Morris: I'd sniffed a few lines earlier that night and had a few shots of Vodka.

Det. Green: Is everything that you've said here today truthful and honest?

Cindy Morris: Yes, I swear it is.

Det. Green: OK. Thank you for your time, patience, and honesty today.

Detective Hall switched the tape recorder off after listening to that interview.

"Detective Green was right. Symone was the killer in Detective Boatman's assassination, but why didn't any of this come out? Why am I just now hearing this?" Detective Hall put the tape and the folder to the side, and then continued to pack Detective Green's property before exiting Green's office.

***

Symone sat in her office on the docks, looking at a globe of the world, talking to Halo and Slim Boogie.

"Slim, now that you're back, I'm gonna let you run the docks. Halo's got the jewelry stores."

"Symone, it's crazy. You did it. The last thing I remember we was war with the LaCross Family, and we didn't have nothing. Now you have an empire."

"No, Slim Boogie, we have a Bloodstone Dynasty. Oppositions came with the course of blood. Our soldiers stayed strong and solid as a diamond, and together we built our dynasty. Now look, we are one of the most feared families in New York. One thing Jamila always taught me is that motherfuckers only respect violence."

"Rose, so when do we start expecting our new shipments of heroin from Glenn Pauliani?"

"The shipments will start coming in this week, Halo, to Slim Boogie on the docks. Slim, when the shipments come in, you get in touch with Perk-G so that he can do his part. I want y'all both to remember, this is just one stepping stone to a new level that we're going to." Symone walked to her desk, took a seat, and lit a Black and Mild without saying another word because there was nothing else to be said.

Chapter Forty-Seven

Jamila and Tasha walked into the room, and looked around at everyone sitting at the table. Everyone stood up when they noticed Jamila's presence.

"Y'all can take your seats. As of last week, everyone should know that Tasha is my number two. Y'all will give her the same respect that you would give me. I know that y'all have questions about what happened to Lorenzo. I know some of you loved and respected him. He was your homeboy, but nobody loved him more than me, nobody respected him more than me. He was by my side before the LaCross Family was a thought, but nobody, I repeat this, nobody is bigger than the LaCross Family. My rules abide by him just like they do for everybody else. The first time you show a sign of disloyalty, you fuck up, you die. We have lost too many honest, loyal soldiers over the years, all of whom bled and lost their lives over our family. Lorenzo lied. He betrayed us all. He started a spark that turned into a fire between us and the Rose Family. Symone Rose never betrayed us. Lorenzo lied against her, and cost us family members to an unnecessary war. That wasn't his first act of betrayal. It was his second act. His first act was against me for many years, and his second act of betrayal brought out the truth about the first act. I need to be able to trust you guys in the hardest situations, and I need for you all to trust my decisions. I want you all to take a look at each other around this table. There's nobody sitting in here that's got a friend. When I give the order to kill, you will die by the hands of the man sitting next to you or across from you. I trusted Muscle with a very hard and difficult decision. Because of his loyalty and trust in me, he didn't question my judgement. He simply did what he was told. Because of his actions, he is now the third highest ranking member of the LaCross Family. Muscle stand up."

Jamila looked at Tasha and nodded.

Tasha walked over to Muscle and handed him a small black jewelry box. Muscle opened the box and looked at the diamond ring inside. Everyone was looking at Muscle. "The red diamond in your ring stands for the blood you spilled for this family. The blue diamond stands for your honesty in this family, and the clear diamond stands for your position in this family. Tonight, we celebrate a collective victory. I want y'all all to remember we stand on the foundation of love, trust and loyalty. No one will speak to me directly. You'll go through the chains of command, through Muscle and Tasha. You will speak with Muscle, and Muscle will speak with Tasha, then Tasha will speak with me. With that being said, enjoy your gathering." Jamila looked at everybody one last time before she and Tasha walked out of the room.

Chapter Forty-Eight

Detective Hall knocked on Chief Tadem's office door and waited on the other side until he heard: "Come in". When he walked into his office, Chief Tadem was sitting behind his desk, smoking a cigar.

"Tell me, Hall, to what do I owe the honor of this visit?" Chief Tadem said, as he leaned back in his chair.

"I want to ask you the truth about something."

"It depends on what you wanna know."

"Was Green murdered because he was trying to find out the truth or was he murdered because you were trying to cover up the identity of someone else?"

"I don't know what you're talking about, Hall."

"Are you sure you don't know what I'm talking about, Chief?"

"Are you in here questioning me, detective? I'm starting to think you've forgotten your place."

Detective Hall licked his lips and nodded twice as he looked at him.

"You know what, Chief? I didn't forget my place, but Green lost his life trying to bring a cop killer to justice. A wife lost her husband, and children lost their father."

"Like I said before, I'm not trying to cover up for nobody, and Detective Green knew the bed he was making before he laid down in it."

Detective Hall stood up and looked at the Chief. Tadem kept smoking casually on his cigar.

"One thing I know about proper procedures, protocol states that everything that a detective does must be signed off on, and all evidence and statements must be brought back to the Chief for a review. Those are the guidelines for any investigation."

"So what's your point, Hall? Get to it fast."

Hall reached inside his jacket, pulled out the manilla envelope and slammed it on Chief Tadem's desk.

"That's my point right there. Cindy Morris described Symone Rose to the tee. She gave Detective Green full details of Detective

Boatman's assassination. She was there that night. She witnessed everything. And that envelope on your desk gives full details as it happened, from how many shots she heard, from the fluid being poured on him, from the old lady being killed down the street to the car Symone fled away from the scene. I went and got the autopsy report of his assassination. So, you want me to get to the point? He showed you his witness statement, and you heard this audio tape and you refused to sign off on it for whatever reasons. That's why it was never logged into evidence. So you're claiming you're not trying to cover up for Symone Rose? Then that means that the shit is bigger than you, Chief Tadem. That means you're a small mouse about to get caught in a big rat trap, because whoever got their foot on your neck—I'm gunning for them, and let me tell you this: Hell will freeze over, and my mother will be a bitch before I go out bad and let a motherfucker kill me. Because Symone Rose is gonna sit her black ass down, she's gonna look at twelve jurors, one judge, one D.A., and my black ass in the audience—and you can take that to the bank." Detective Hall looked at Chief Tadem one last time before walking out of Chief Tadem's office, slamming the door behind him.

Chapter Forty-Nine

Symone walked into the casino with Halo in tow. Iceman came walking down the stairs to meet them. Iceman walked up to Symone and gave her a kiss on both cheeks.

"Ms. Rose, why didn't you tell me you were coming by? Why the surprise?"

"It's not a surprise. I just didn't feel the need to call. How are things going here?"

"Everything is going good, Ms. Rose. Our numbers are up. People are gambling. The girls are doing what they're supposed to be doing. Perk-G came by and dropped me off seven packages. The girls are loving it, and the customers are buying it."

"It sounds like everything is a win-win for us, and everything Glenn said about his product held up to its expectations. How many girls did Pistol bring by here?"

"He brought eight girls here."

"Take me and introduce me to them."

"Come on, right this way. They're all in the VIP section, in the private rooms."

Symone watched the floor as they made their way through the crowd. She looked at the crowd around the blackjack table and the poker table, as they made their way to the back of the casino. Iceman walked them into a room with double-sided windows as he showed her two of the girls entertaining a customer. Symone watched as one of the girls kissed the side of the customer's neck while the other girl performed oral sex on him.

"How long do they normally entertain their customers in these rooms?"

"It depends on the customer. I charge three hundred an hour for each one of these rooms."

"How long he been back there with them so far?"

"Let me check the log-in back. It says here, he's been back there with them for two hours now."

"Come on. Show me the rest of the girls now." As they walked into another room, Symone watched as an older white gentleman snorted a small pile of cocaine off a girl's breast. On the table beside them was a quarter brick of cocaine.

"Iceman, how much did you charge him for *that* on the table, and how long have they been in the room together?"

"He's actually been here since last night about eight o'clock, so he's been here for twenty-one hours, so that's six thousand three hundred dollars that he's spent on the room alone, and we charged him ten thousand for the product that he's enjoying. Do you care to see what the rest of the girls are doing?"

"Yes, let's go and see one more." When Symone walked into the room, she noticed a familiar face. Iceman and Halo looked at her as she stared at the man while he was being pleased.

"Iceman, do you know who that man is right there?"

"Honestly, no, but it says in the logbook that he's been here for an hour and a half."

"His name is Anthony Tadem, and he's the Chief of Police. Call our girl out of there. I want to speak with him. I want to know why he's here."

Iceman knocked on the door two times before opening it up. Chief Tadem looked at Iceman as he walked through the door.

"I'm sorry for the inconvenience, but we have another lady that we'd like to bring into the room with you." Iceman opened the door just wide enough to let the girl out of the room.

"Again, I'm sorry for the inconvenience. Just give us a few minutes and we'll have another lady come in to entertain you, sir."

"No problem, as long as she's as beautiful and fine as the one that's walking out of here now."

Chief Tadem was taking off his shirt when the door opened and Symone walked into his room.

"No need for that, Chief Tadem. You can keep your shirt on. This isn't going to take long. So, tell me, why are you here? And don't tell me it's for the girls."

"No. No. I'm not here for the girls. I'm here because we have a problem with an officer who is trying to put you under investigation for the murder of Detective Deontay Boatman."

"You know what, Chief Tadem? Get undressed. I want every-thing off of you."

"Ms. Rose, I'm not wearing a wire."

"And a rat will tell you it never bit the cheese. Get undressed."

Chief Tadem was about to say something, but stopped when he saw Iceman reaching for his gun. He stood up and complied with what Symone said. Symone watched as Chief Tadem stripped all the way down to his briefs. Iceman walked over, picked up his clothes and checked them for a wire.

"So, tell me now, Chief Tadem, who is this officer who's trying to put me under investigation?"

"His name is Hall, and he's a friend of Detective Green's. That's not all, though. There's a witness, and she can identify you. She saw everything. She even heard you when you said something about Lorenzo."

"Give me the name of this witness, the detective's name, and tell me where I can find them."

Chief Tadem reached into his pants pocket and pulled out a piece of paper with the names and addresses on them. Symone reached for the piece of paper as Chief Tadem handed it to her, and she looked at the names and addresses.

"Chief Tadem, I'll be in touch." As Symone and Iceman turned to leave the room, Chief Tadem stopped them.

"Ms. Rose, Special Director Smith of the F.B.I told me that my department has a lot of loose strings."

"Special Director Smith of the F.B.I. is right, and you—Chief Tadem—are starting to become a loose string." As they walked out the door, the lady that was entertaining Chief Tadem went back into the room before the door closed.

"So what now, Rose? Where do we go from here?" asked Ice-man.

"We find out who Cindy Morris is, and take her on a ride that she won't come back from. Tell Pistol that Detective Hall needs to have a face-to-face talk with Detective Deontay Boatman."

***

Jamila walked into the warehouse with a paper bag in her hand. She walked up to the man sitting at the table with his back turned to her.

"Hello, Mr. Cap. How are you today? I'm glad you could make it."

"When the Queen Don calls, I come."

"Well, this is for you, as promised." Jamila handed him the paper bag.

"There's one-hundred thousand dollars in this paper bag as promised."

Cap took the bag and looked inside of it.

"I have another job for you."

"Who is it this time?"

"Does it matter?"

"No, it doesn't."

"Good. Here are the names and addresses."

Cap took the piece of paper and read the names out loud.

"Cindy Morris, Detective Hall, and Chief Anthony Tadem." Young Cap placed the piece of paper on the table after calling out the names.

"Yes. I need all of them taken care of, in your style of expertise." Jamila watched as Young Cap smiled at her with a crooked grin. He picked the paper bag up off the table and looked at her.

"I'll be in touch."

Jamila watched as Cap walked out of the warehouse. She pulled out her phone and made a phone call. After two rings, Tasha picked up.

"Tasha, get in touch with Rose, and let her know that her itch has been scratched."

After saying that, she hung up the phone, and said to herself: "A favor for a favor."

The End

Lock Down Publications and Ca$h Presents assisted publishing packages.

BASIC PACKAGE $499

Editing

Cover Design

Formatting

UPGRADED PACKAGE $800

Typing

Editing

Cover Design

Formatting

ADVANCE PACKAGE $1,200

Typing

Editing

Cover Design

Formatting

Copyright registration

Proofreading

Upload book to Amazon

LDP SUPREME PACKAGE $1,500

Typing

Editing

Cover Design

Formatting

Copyright registration

Proofreading

Set up Amazon account

Upload book to Amazon

Advertise on LDP Amazon and Facebook page

***Other services available upon request. Additional charges may apply

Lock Down Publications

P.O. Box 944

Stockbridge, GA 30281-9998

Phone # 470 303-9761

Submission Guideline

Submit the first three chapters of your completed manuscript to ldpsubmissions@gmail.com, subject line: Your book's title. The manuscript must be in a .doc file and sent as an attachment. Document should be in Times New Roman, double spaced and in size 12 font. Also, provide your synopsis and full contact information. If sending multiple submissions, they must each be in a separate email.

Have a story but no way to send it electronically? You can still submit to LDP/Ca$h Presents. Send in the first three chapters, written or typed, of your completed manuscript to:

LDP: Submissions Dept
Po Box 944
Stockbridge, Ga 30281

DO NOT send original manuscript. Must be a duplicate.

Provide your synopsis and a cover letter containing your full contact information.

Thanks for considering LDP and Ca$h Presents.

NEW RELEASES

CUM FOR ME by SUGAR E. WALLZ
THE BRICK MAN 3 by KING RIO
THE PLUG OF LIL MEXICO by CHRIS GREEN
THE STREETS STAINED MY SOUL 3 by MAR-
CELLUS ALLEN
KING OF THE TRENCHES 2 by GHOST & TRA-
NAY ADAMS
MOB TIES 5 by SAYNOMORE

KINGPIN KILLAZ IV

STREET KINGS III

PAID IN BLOOD III

CARTEL KILLAZ IV

DOPE GODS III

Hood Rich

SINS OF A HUSTLA II

ASAD

RICH $AVAGE II

MONEY IN THE GRAVE II

By Martell Troublesome Bolden

YAYO V

Bred In The Game 2

S. Allen

CREAM III

By Yolanda Moore

SON OF A DOPE FIEND III

HEAVEN GOT A GHETTO II

By Renta

LOYALTY AIN'T PROMISED III

By Keith Williams

I'M NOTHING WITHOUT HIS LOVE II

SINS OF A THUG II

TO THE THUG I LOVED BEFORE II

By Monet Dragun

QUIET MONEY IV

EXTENDED CLIP III

THUG LIFE IV

By **Trai'Quan**

THE STREETS MADE ME IV

By **Larry D. Wright**

IF YOU CROSS ME ONCE II

By **Anthony Fields**

THE STREETS WILL NEVER CLOSE II

By **K'ajji**

HARD AND RUTHLESS III

THE BILLIONAIRE BENTLEYS II

Von Diesel

KILLA KOUNTY II

By **Khufu**

MONEY GAME III

By **Smoove Dolla**

JACK BOYZ VERSUS DOPE BOYZ

By **Romell Tukes**

MURDA WAS THE CASE II

Elijah R. Freeman

THE STREETS NEVER LET GO II

By **Robert Baptiste**

AN UNFORESEEN LOVE III

By **Meesha**

KING OF THE TRENCHES III
by **GHOST & TRANAY ADAMS**

MONEY MAFIA II

LOYAL TO THE SOIL II

By **Jibril Williams**

QUEEN OF THE ZOO II

By **Black Migo**

THE BRICK MAN IV

By **King Rio**

VICIOUS LOYALTY II

SAYNOMORE

By Kingpen
A GANGSTA'S PAIN II
By J-Blunt
CONFESSIONS OF A JACKBOY III
By Nicholas Lock
GRIMEY WAYS II
By Ray Vinci

Available Now

RESTRAINING ORDER **I & II**
By **CA$H & Coffee**
LOVE KNOWS NO BOUNDARIES **I II & III**
By **Coffee**
RAISED AS A GOON I, II, III & IV
BRED BY THE SLUMS I, II, III
BLAST FOR ME I & II
ROTTEN TO THE CORE I II III
A BRONX TALE I, II, III
DUFFLE BAG CARTEL I II III IV V VI
HEARTLESS GOON I II III IV V
A SAVAGE DOPEBOY I II
DRUG LORDS I II III
CUTTHROAT MAFIA I II

KING OF THE TRENCHES

By **Ghost**

LAY IT DOWN **I & II**

LAST OF A DYING BREED I II

BLOOD STAINS OF A SHOTTA I & II III

By **Jamaica**

LOYAL TO THE GAME I II III

LIFE OF SIN I, II III

By **TJ & Jelissa**

BLOODY COMMAS I & II

SKI MASK CARTEL I II & III

KING OF NEW YORK I II,III IV V

RISE TO POWER I II III

COKE KINGS I II III IV V

BORN HEARTLESS I II III IV

KING OF THE TRAP I II

By **T.J. Edwards**

IF LOVING HIM IS WRONG…I & II

LOVE ME EVEN WHEN IT HURTS I II III

By **Jelissa**

WHEN THE STREETS CLAP BACK I & II III

THE HEART OF A SAVAGE I II III

MONEY MAFIA

LOYAL TO THE SOIL

By **Jibril Williams**

A DISTINGUISHED THUG STOLE MY HEART I II & III

LOVE SHOULDN'T HURT I II III IV

RENEGADE BOYS I II III IV

PAID IN KARMA I II III

SAVAGE STORMS I II

SAYNOMORE

AN UNFORESEEN LOVE I II

By **Meesha**

A GANGSTER'S CODE I &, II III

A GANGSTER'S SYN I II III

THE SAVAGE LIFE I II III

CHAINED TO THE STREETS I II III

BLOOD ON THE MONEY I II III

A GANGSTA'S PAIN

By J-Blunt

PUSH IT TO THE LIMIT

By **Bre' Hayes**

BLOOD OF A BOSS **I, II, III, IV, V**

SHADOWS OF THE GAME

TRAP BASTARD

By **Askari**

THE STREETS BLEED MURDER **I, II & III**

THE HEART OF A GANGSTA I II& III

By **Jerry Jackson**

CUM FOR ME I II III IV V VI VII VIII

An **LDP Erotica Collaboration**

BRIDE OF A HUSTLA **I II & II**

THE FETTI GIRLS **I, II& III**

CORRUPTED BY A GANGSTA I, II III, IV

BLINDED BY HIS LOVE

THE PRICE YOU PAY FOR LOVE I, II ,III

DOPE GIRL MAGIC I II III

By **Destiny Skai**

WHEN A GOOD GIRL GOES BAD

By **Adrienne**

THE COST OF LOYALTY I II III

By Kweli

A GANGSTER'S REVENGE **I II III & IV**

THE BOSS MAN'S DAUGHTERS I II III IV V

A SAVAGE LOVE **I & II**

BAE BELONGS TO ME I II

A HUSTLER'S DECEIT I, II, III

WHAT BAD BITCHES DO I, II, III

SOUL OF A MONSTER I II III

KILL ZONE

A DOPE BOY'S QUEEN I II III

By **Aryanna**

A KINGPIN'S AMBITON

A KINGPIN'S AMBITION **II**

I MURDER FOR THE DOUGH

By **Ambitious**

TRUE SAVAGE I II III IV V VI VII

DOPE BOY MAGIC I, II, III

MIDNIGHT CARTEL I II III

CITY OF KINGZ I II

NIGHTMARE ON SILENT AVE

THE PLUG OF LIL MEXICO II

By **Chris Green**

A DOPEBOY'S PRAYER

By **Eddie "Wolf" Lee**

THE KING CARTEL **I, II & III**

By **Frank Gresham**

THESE NIGGAS AIN'T LOYAL **I, II & III**

By **Nikki Tee**

GANGSTA SHYT **I II &III**

SAYNOMORE

By **CATO**
THE ULTIMATE BETRAYAL
By **Phoenix**
BOSS'N UP **I , II & III**
By **Royal Nicole**
I LOVE YOU TO DEATH
By **Destiny J**
I RIDE FOR MY HITTA
I STILL RIDE FOR MY HITTA
By **Misty Holt**
LOVE & CHASIN' PAPER
By **Qay Crockett**
TO DIE IN VAIN
SINS OF A HUSTLA
By **ASAD**
BROOKLYN HUSTLAZ
By **Boogsy Morina**
BROOKLYN ON LOCK I & II
By **Sonovia**
GANGSTA CITY
By **Teddy Duke**
A DRUG KING AND HIS DIAMOND I & II III
A DOPEMAN'S RICHES
HER MAN, MINE'S TOO I, II
CASH MONEY HO'S
THE WIFEY I USED TO BE I II
By Nicole Goosby
TRAPHOUSE KING **I II & III**
KINGPIN KILLAZ I II III
STREET KINGS I II

PAID IN BLOOD **I II**

CARTEL KILLAZ I II III

DOPE GODS I II

By **Hood Rich**

LIPSTICK KILLAH **I, II, III**

CRIME OF PASSION I II & III

FRIEND OR FOE I II III

By **Mimi**

STEADY MOBBN' **I, II, III**

THE STREETS STAINED MY SOUL I II III

By **Marcellus Allen**

WHO SHOT YA **I, II, III**

SON OF A DOPE FIEND I II

HEAVEN GOT A GHETTO

Renta

GORILLAZ IN THE BAY **I II III IV**

TEARS OF A GANGSTA I II

3X KRAZY I II

STRAIGHT BEAST MODE

DE'KARI

TRIGGADALE I II III

MURDAROBER WAS THE CASE

Elijah R. Freeman

GOD BLESS THE TRAPPERS I, II, III

THESE SCANDALOUS STREETS I, II, III

FEAR MY GANGSTA I, II, III IV, V

THESE STREETS DON'T LOVE NOBODY I, II

BURY ME A G I, II, III, IV, V

A GANGSTA'S EMPIRE I, II, III, IV

THE DOPEMAN'S BODYGAURD I II

SAYNOMORE

THE REALEST KILLAZ I II III
THE LAST OF THE OGS I II III
Tranay Adams
THE STREETS ARE CALLING
Duquie Wilson
MARRIED TO A BOSS II III
By Destiny Skai & Chris Green
KINGZ OF THE GAME I II III IV V VI
Playa Ray
SLAUGHTER GANG I II III
RUTHLESS HEART I II III
By Willie Slaughter
FUK SHYT
By Blakk Diamond
DON'T F#CK WITH MY HEART I II
By Linnea
ADDICTED TO THE DRAMA I II III
IN THE ARM OF HIS BOSS II
By Jamila
YAYO I II III IV
A SHOOTER'S AMBITION I II
BRED IN THE GAME
By S. Allen
TRAP GOD I II III
RICH $AVAGE
MONEY IN THE GRAVE I II
By Martell Troublesome Bolden
FOREVER GANGSTA
GLOCKS ON SATIN SHEETS I II
By Adrian Dulan

212

TOE TAGZ I II III

LEVELS TO THIS SHYT I II

By Ah'Million

KINGPIN DREAMS I II III

By Paper Boi Rari

CONFESSIONS OF A GANGSTA I II III IV

CONFESSIONS OF A JACKBOY I II

By Nicholas Lock

I'M NOTHING WITHOUT HIS LOVE

SINS OF A THUG

TO THE THUG I LOVED BEFORE

A GANGSTA SAVED XMAS

By Monet Dragun

CAUGHT UP IN THE LIFE I II III

THE STREETS NEVER LET GO

By Robert Baptiste

NEW TO THE GAME I II III

MONEY, MURDER & MEMORIES I II III

By **Malik D. Rice**

LIFE OF A SAVAGE I II III

A GANGSTA'S QUR'AN I II III

MURDA SEASON I II III

GANGLAND CARTEL I II III

CHI'RAQ GANGSTAS I II III

KILLERS ON ELM STREET I II III

JACK BOYZ N DA BRONX I II III

A DOPEBOY'S DREAM I II III

By **Romell Tukes**

LOYALTY AIN'T PROMISED I II

By Keith Williams

SAYNOMORE

QUIET MONEY I II III
THUG LIFE I II III
EXTENDED CLIP I II
By **Trai'Quan**
THE STREETS MADE ME I II III
By **Larry D. Wright**
THE ULTIMATE SACRIFICE I, II, III, IV, V, VI
KHADIFI
IF YOU CROSS ME ONCE
ANGEL I II
IN THE BLINK OF AN EYE
By **Anthony Fields**
THE LIFE OF A HOOD STAR
By Ca$h & Rashia Wilson
THE STREETS WILL NEVER CLOSE
By K'ajji
CREAM I II
By Yolanda Moore
NIGHTMARES OF A HUSTLA I II III
By King Dream
CONCRETE KILLA I II
VICIOUS LOYALTY
By Kingpen
HARD AND RUTHLESS I II
MOB TOWN 251
THE BILLIONAIRE BENTLEYS
By Von Diesel
GHOST MOB
Stilloan Robinson
MOB TIES I II III IV V

214

By SayNoMore

BODYMORE MURDERLAND I II III

By Delmont Player

FOR THE LOVE OF A BOSS

By C. D. Blue

MOBBED UP I II III IV

THE BRICK MAN I II III

By King Rio

KILLA KOUNTY

By Khufu

MONEY GAME I II

By Smoove Dolla

A GANGSTA'S KARMA I II

By FLAME

KING OF THE TRENCHES I II

by **GHOST & TRANAY ADAMS**

QUEEN OF THE ZOO

By **Black Migo**

GRIMEY WAYS

By Ray Vinci

XMAS WITH AN ATL SHOOTER

By Ca$h & Destiny Skai

BOOKS BY LDP'S CEO, CA$H

TRUST IN NO MAN

TRUST IN NO MAN 2

TRUST IN NO MAN 3

BONDED BY BLOOD

SHORTY GOT A THUG

THUGS CRY

THUGS CRY 2

THUGS CRY 3

TRUST NO BITCH

TRUST NO BITCH 2

TRUST NO BITCH 3

TIL MY CASKET DROPS

RESTRAINING ORDER

RESTRAINING ORDER 2

IN LOVE WITH A CONVICT

LIFE OF A HOOD STAR

XMAS WITH AN ATL SHOOTER